i am
free

regina bartley

I AM FREE

Copyright © 2015 Regina Bartley

All rights reserved

This book is a work of fiction. Names, characters, places, and incidents are either the product of the author's imagination or are used fictitiously. Any similarity between actual persons, living or dead, is purely coincidental. Any uses of locales, or events are used fictitiously.

Cover Design: Sprinkles on Top Studio

Formatted by: Ready, Set, Edit

Dedication

For my niece Kelsey, who has taught me so many things.

You've taught me that unconditional love is for everyone.

You've taught me to see beauty in all things.

You've taught me that friendship is boundless.

You've taught me to fight for what I want.

K- Kind

E- Exquisite

L- Loving

S- Strong

E- Extraordinary

Y- You are so many things, but most of all you are YOU!

I love you!

Prologue

Grace- Fifteen Years Old

My faith was the reason I kept from killing my father. His fists were heavy, and served their purpose. They were forceful, and though my mother witnessed, she never said a cross word or any word in my defense. I sometimes doubted her love for me. She was just scared, I told myself. She knew that if she spoke up, that her punishment would be far worse than mine, at least that was the excuse that I told myself. The one I repeated over and over to cover up her unexplainable parenting skills. Hidden behind that apron was a woman that was just as frightened as me, but despite it all she still loved him.

And somewhere deep down inside, I despised her for it.

From the moment I was old enough to remember, I wanted to run away. Not because I hated my life. Not

1

because I hated my Mother or my older brother Thomas. I had love for them, somewhere hidden, no matter how hollow they were inside. I loved my home, and our farm, the entirety of it all. Our way of life was different, but I never dreamed of anything more. The only reason that I ever wanted to leave was because of him. My father.

The summer after my fifteenth birthday I almost did it. If I could have walked or talked after his beating then I would have.

Early morning sunrises in Oklahoma were picture perfect, and that morning was no different. I made sure to be up extra early. As in before the rooster crowed. I knew it was going to be a hot one, and I had one hour before I had to begin my chores. Never once had I considered defying my father, but I wanted to go swimming and he'd said no. He always said no. Girls weren't supposed to wear suits that bared their skin for anyone to see. It was preposterous, and quite surely the biggest sin. I was allowed to wade in the water but had to wear my skirt. There was absolutely no fun in that.

I knew the risk when I snuck down to the pond that morning, but thought I'd never get caught. I was extra quiet and was sure that I'd covered all of my tracks. Ducking low behind the shed, and making sure to walk along the far side of the tree line so that I wouldn't stir up the animals. My father never went down to the pond. It was too far of a hike for his bad leg.

I had it all figured out. I would not get my hair wet, and I would leave my dry clothes on the dock so that I could put them on once I was done. The plan seemed flawless, but what I didn't suspect was someone else catching me. The pond backed up to the Turner farm, and Katie Turner and I had never gotten along. She was a snobby piece of work who hated me with a passion. I never understood why, but it only made me dislike her worse. Her, and her beautiful tan legs that she showed off every chance she got. She never gave me a chance to be her friend, never tried to like me. She made fun of me and made sure to make my life a living hell.

Splashing around in the water, I hadn't heard her sneak up to the dock. I was too busy relishing in my morning of fun. I was unaware of her cruel intentions.

She'd taken my dry clothes and ran home with them. Leaving me with nothing. I'd try to call after her, but was too late. The only clothing covering my skin was my bra, a white tank top, and my underwear. My father was going to kill me. I knew that he was.

We weren't really the religious type of family. I mean we believed in God, but we didn't go to church. Dad said that the only organized religion that we needed was prayer before supper. My dad had his own set of rules for us to follow. He was a strict man, and he firmly believed that a woman's body was not to be tampered with or to be seen by the eyes of anyone other than her husband. We wore long skirts and collared shirts. We were allowed to wear short sleeves if the weather was hot, but only then. We never wore makeup or did anything to make ourselves appear older. It was unheard of. I never cared much about those rules. I followed them, because I had to. I never complained, at least not to my father's face. It was all I had ever known.

But sometimes he went overboard, and this was one of those times.

I crept back to the house knowing full well that anyone who would see me would be able to see right through the clothes I was wearing. I had no choice. I had to get back.

The bottom of my long blond hair was dripping wear the ends had touched water. My hands could only cover so much, and when I stepped up to the back door my father was awake and staring at me through the screen with cold eyes.

"Shed now!" he demanded.

His stare alone was enough to scare me, but that voice. It haunted my dreams.

My head hung low as I tiptoed on the dry ground all the way to the shed. I could feel his eyes burning into me from behind all though I couldn't see them. The aluminum door made a creaking nose as it opened, and a loud banging noise when it slammed shut.

"You have defied me child, and you'll take your punishment." The sweat dripped from the creases in his forehead and the whites of his eyes were devil red.

"I'm sorry," I started to say with a shaky voice.

"Don't speak!" He yelled. "Your body is not to be seen, and I will make sure that you never want to show it again."

I started to sink to my knees in fear, but he screamed for me to stand up straighter.

Many times I had taken a beaten from my father, but never was he this mad. Never had he looked at me with such disgust. I feared for my life, as I stood there barefoot on the hard ground.

He grabbed the first tool he could find hanging on the wall. The rake. He twisted it around so that the metal end was in his hands and the wooden handle was sticking out into the air as if he were holding a bat. "Turn around." He ordered.

I knew what he was about to do, but in my mind I had hoped that he wouldn't be too hard on me.

I was wrong.

The first hit to the back of my legs took me to the ground. It completely knocked me off of my feet, and though I screamed it did no good. I was barely able to catch my breath.

"Stand up!" He yelled again, and I did as I was asked. Defying him would only make it worse.

I knew when the next hit was coming because I could hear the whoosh of air as he swung the rake towards my body.

Over and over, he hit me.

Each time my body went to the ground. The screaming played like a broken record in my head. At times it didn't even sound like me. I sounded like a little girl. Not the teenage girl that I was.

The pain was so bad that I blacked out a couple of times. But the next swing would make me conscious again.

I couldn't get up. I couldn't move. My body was glued face down into the dirt floor of the shed. Sobs racked my body, and I shook so much that my shoulders banged against the floor.

No one came. Not my mother or my brother.

I never tried to fight back or get up because it wouldn't have done any good. There was no way I could even walk. The bones in my legs from my knees down felt like they were shattered. I knew they weren't, but it felt like it.

When he was finally out of breath the beating stopped. I thought it was over. Usually when he was wore out; he would break something and slam the door on his way out.

I was wrong again.

Just when I thought it was over, I felt cold sticks just below my neck. Then pressure. The metal end of the rake was being dug into my skin, full force. He scraped the tips from my shoulder blades to my butt bone. What little clothing I was wearing tore into shreds around me, and I tried to cry out. I tried. The sound was mute though. It never left my body, but shrilled in my brain.

The warm wetness of blood covered my back. I could feel it leaking down my sides. There was a slam of the door, but that was the last thing I remembered when the darkness took over.

My back must have quit bleeding at some point, because when I woke up and moved mere inches it felt dried and scabbed. Like my back was one big sore. I had lain there for hours I assumed, because my legs wouldn't move. My brain knew that they needed to, but my body wouldn't listen.

Finally sometime in the night my mother showed up with some aspirins and a glass of water. My father had gone to bed so she came to get me. She helped me too my feet and then to my bed, which took us forever. She didn't ask if I needed a doctor, because that was out of the question. She barely even looked at me. Probably for fear that she might actually feel an ounce of guilt for leaving me lying there in that condition all day. I could've been dead and no one would have known, or cared.

Once I learned that I could walk on my aching legs, I knew that nothing was broken. But it may has well have been. It hurt just the same, and if nothing else, my heart was.

My heart was broken, and what little thread of love I had for my father was gone completely. I'd never care for that man again, no matter what.

The evil man that called himself my father would never be. He would always be a monster in my eyes. He could never live up to those words, and I hoped that one day he would meet his match. That someone would teach him a lesson that he'd never forget.

When my mother waited for me to put my legs up onto my bed, she finally looked at me but only because I made her. I glared so deep at her eyes that they were forced to look in my direction.

She said, "You can take tomorrow off from chores since you're sick." Then she walked out my door.

That was it. I could have one lousy day off from chores.

Yippy.

There was no remorse or love, only one smart remark. She wouldn't even offer to help me clean up.

I would've liked to have said screw you, but I didn't have the energy or the will power.

That was the night that I realized that she was just as heartless as he was, and I vowed that I would leave that place as soon as I turned eighteen. All the times that I wanted to runaway never compared to this one. Soon it would be real. I would get out of this mess of a life, and never look back.

And that was what I did.

i am free

1

Grace

The morning of my eighteenth birthday my mom made a big breakfast, same as she had in years before. Everyone sat around the kitchen table to eat before the sun even came up. Mom told me I could have the day off from my chores, and even though I could tell dad was against it he still nodded his head and agreed. The frown lines on his forehead had grown deeper with age and anger. I tried not to stare, because his eyes were always filled with such hatred and evilness. He could make you flinch with one look. I glanced around the room, anywhere but there.

I knew that things would be a little bit different once I turned eighteen, and became an adult. But being a prisoner in this lifestyle wasn't one of those changes. If they had their way, I'd be stuck there doing chores for the rest of my life. I'd have no friends, and would know nothing of the life outside of this town.

My dad was going to see to it that I always obeyed his every command. The only difference now was that I was old enough to date. Not that I had any plans to do it. Plus there would be a long list of rules and guidelines that would follow right along with it. He would demand that the boy be from our community, a hard worker, and someone with strong values and morals. In other words, he'd want me to be with a younger version of himself.

Right?

Like that was going to happen.

His old fashioned lifestyle was too much for me, way too much. I wouldn't settle for anyone unless they were his complete opposite. Things had changed over the last one hundred years. People didn't court anymore. My mom didn't leave me completely out in the cold when she taught me my studies, but there were tons of things that I'd be figuring out on my own. I could only hope that she wasn't filling my head full of lies though, because after tonight I would be a member of society. Not just a lovely member of this household. Despite my lack of social skills, I felt like my grasp on reality or what lay beyond the twenty-mile radius of town was crystal clear.

I wasn't about to spend another night in this house, under this roof, with that man. I peeked up from my fork once and saw him glaring at my mother. She just sat there like her normal robot self. Smiling as if she didn't notice. I wanted to storm off from the table, but I knew that would only mean pain for me. It was all the more reason for me to get out.

The next eighteen hours couldn't come fast enough.

That night I packed one duffel bag of my things, and left my home in Oklahoma.

Finally.

I had saved the ten dollars that my aunt had sent me in a birthday card every year since I was old enough to read them. She would never know how much that money truly saved me. It was the only money I had, and it was enough to purchase a one-way bus ticket to Colorado.

Several months before, I had written to her and asked if I could come stay with her. She wouldn't deny me. I knew that. She despised my father almost as much as I did. She would take pride in lending me a helping hand so that I could leave.

When she sent me my most recent birthday card that arrived just days ago, she'd written something so simple inside. The words –Happy Birthday Grace; my home is yours. Like I said, the words were simple, but it was the finality that I'd longed for, and a silent agreement between the two of us. I knew what I had to do.

My bus ticket was purchased. That was the easy part. Getting out of my house without getting caught would be another story.

Tossing my bag over my shoulder, I looked around my bedroom one last time. It was the only thing about that life that I wanted to remember. It was the only thing that I could call my own. I didn't have to share it, and when I wanted to be alone I knew that I could. My fingers grazed over the yellow blanket that my grandmother made. I wished that I could take it with me, but getting out was my main focus. There was limited room in my small bag, and so I couldn't be picky. Necessities only.

I didn't bother closing my bedroom door, when I walked out. My white Keds made zero noise as I tiptoed down the hall. There was only darkness, outside of the moonlight shining through the window in the kitchen, but I didn't need the light. These walls had been mine for eighteen years, and I knew every crease, crack, and crevice. I knew just where to step to avoid the noises that the hardwood floor made. I knew that there was a piece of trim that lay loose where the hallway met the kitchen, and if you weren't careful, it would catch your toe or the hem of your skirt.

When I reached the back door, it was clear that I had made it. If anyone found me there where I stood, I'd just run like the wind. Never look back.

I grabbed an apple out of the basket that sat on the kitchen counter for my trip. I slipped it into the opening of my bag, and then carefully opened the back door hoping like hell that it wouldn't be loud.

Luck was on my side.

When it latched closed, I held my breath until I reached the end of the driveway. Then held it again until I reached the next drive. Each step towards town made me breathe a little easier. Walking alone in the dark didn't scare me, but picturing my father's face around every bend did.

I hoped that he wouldn't try to come after me. Being eighteen gave me some shred of hope. But he was wicked. I wouldn't put it past him to lay some kind of claim over my life once he found out where I was. All I wanted was the freedom, and no matter how many miles I put between the two of us I wondered if I'd ever really be free.

The edge of town was eerily quiet and pleasant. For miles all I saw was emptiness and the night air was still warm against my skin. Leaving at nighttime was the smartest thing for me to get a fresh start. No one seemed to be creeping around, so I wouldn't risk the chance of someone seeing me. At least not anyone I knew. The folks that I had been acquainted with wouldn't be out this time of night. They were early risers.

The streetlights paved the way to the bus stop. My family and I passed by it every time we went to town so I knew exactly where it was. I had purchased my ticket there last Sunday while Mom was inside the grocery store next door.

The sign hung low and very few people stood around as I crept up the wooden steps making my way inside. The station was older and had a pungent smell of Old English polishing oil. It was the same stuff my mother used on the wooden bench that sat on our front porch. Judging by the clock hanging by the door I was just in time, and I wouldn't have to wait long before my bus arrived. Thank goodness.

I was constantly looking over my shoulder in search of him, though I knew he wouldn't be there. And every noise made me jumpy. The poor man that collected my ticket probably thought I had some kind of illness or that I'd forgotten to take my medication. He never said a word though, just a skeptical brow and common politeness.

I took a seat and waited for my bus to come.

Aunt Darcy was expecting me and promised that she wouldn't say one single word to my father. She knew that he was crazy. There was no contact between the two of them besides a Christmas card that came every year. She steered clear of him, like she should. There were times that I wondered if she knew the severity of his temper, but figured if she really knew how bad he was, that she wouldn't say anything. She'd be afraid of him like the rest of us.

i am **free**

She came to visit us once in all the years I could remember. She drove hundreds of miles, and wound up staying for dinner, and leaving soon after. Dad's intense glares, and lack of conversation had everything to do with it. He was not gentle with his words, and sugar coated for no one. Since then all I ever heard from her was –Happy Birthday, in a card.

When I wrote to her back several months ago, I didn't go into full detail about my situation. I only told her that I was leaving and in desperate need of a place to stay. It would be more of a sanctuary then anything. I told her not to write back, because they would be suspicious. So about a week before my birthday I received a new card. Inside it was money of course, and that little note. It was all I needed. She knew that I had no money, but that I would get a job as soon as I arrived.

That frightened the hell out of me. I had no job experience outside of farm work, and my aunt lived nowhere near any farms. She wasn't directly in the city, but close enough. After being home schooled by my mother and graduating when I was only seventeen, I hoped that I would one day be given the opportunity to go to school. College I mean. But I was only kidding myself. I could never afford to go to school, and even if I could what on earth would I study? I knew nothing of the outside world beyond my small town, and from the looks of it –outside the bus window, I was probably in way over my head.

My bag was tucked safely into the small overhead compartment on the bus, and my shoulder bag lay across my lap. The very few belongings I had were mine, and I wanted to keep them as close to me as possible. The seat next to me was empty which was comforting, but the heat mixed with all those bodies made the smell unpleasant. It was musty and smelled like old man cologne mixed with one of those green tree shaped air fresheners. Old pine trees and musk. That about summed it up.

Sometime after the bus started to move I curled up against the armrest. I wrapped my white sweater tightly across my body to keep warm. I didn't want to fall asleep because I was afraid that I would have a terror in front of everyone on the bus. How embarrassing that would be. I tried hard to fight it, but the tiny vibrations of the moving bus were coaxing me into it. The darkness didn't help either.

Unfortunately my eyes couldn't hold out any longer. My heavy eye lids slid closed, and sleep found me too easily.

Thankfully I hadn't been dreaming when I woke some hours later. The screeching of the bus brakes whistled around me, and jolted me awake. The lady that sat a couple of seats over was gathering her things, so I jumped up a little too quickly in my seat. Outside the bus windows was a sign that said Denver Colorado. I knew that I was at my stop. Aunt Darcy lived twenty minutes or so from the city of Denver -just outside of Aurora, but this was the closest stop.

I reached inside the overhead compartment, and grabbed my bag. I straightened my frazzled hair, and patted my long skirt so that the wrinkles weren't crazy then I tossed my bag over my shoulder and made my way towards the front of the bus.

It was dark when I'd first got onto the bus. I could barely see the other passengers. Now, as I was exiting the daylight let me see clearly.

It also made me hope for the darkness again, as everyone stared.

Of course I was a long way from my home, but there was nothing any different about me then the next person. At least on the outside, or from what people could see. I was just plain old me. Boring farm girl hidden behind a long skirt, laced up shoes, and sweaters. Hadn't they ever seen a plain Jane before?

The bright light from the sun nearly made me fall over top of the poor woman in front of me. I had to apologize twelve times to keep her from swinging her purse at my head. Darcy leaped in at just the right time to wrap me in the warmest most inviting hug ever. There was a look on her face telling me not to worry with the old lady.

"Oh, I've missed you." She said. She held me tight. Almost uncomfortably tight when you're not used to being hugged.

"I missed you to." I smiled and laid my head over on her shoulder. She wrapped an arm around me and led us across the street to her car.

Aunt Darcy hadn't changed much at all. She was still very slender with long hair, much like mine. Only darker. She wore makeup and jeans like most of the world, but it wasn't over the top. She was very pretty for an older woman. No husband, and no children, she lived by herself in a two bedroom house in an urban part of town.

I hated imposing on her life, but she accepted me with open arms.

Literally.

"I'm so happy that you are staying with me. We're going to have such a great time together."

"Me too," I answered truthfully. "You won't tell my father right?" I sent a worried glance in her direction from the passenger seat of the car.

"You have my word. I don't plan on talking to that man ever, if I can help it."

I released a pent up breath and watched the building pass by my window. That was all I needed to know. That for once in my life I could feel safe somewhere.

"I am making us a big dinner tonight, and then we can watch movies, or do anything you want. You're eighteen now, so I don't want you to feel like you have to answer to me for any reason. You are my roommate, not my child. I hope you understand that." She explained. Her long red fingernails tapped the steering wheel.

"Yes ma'am. I understand."

"None of that ma'am stuff. It makes me feel old." She smiled.

I returned the smile, and it felt great.

"Want to hear something exciting?"

"Yeah," I waited for her to answer.

"I think I may have found you a job."

"What, seriously?" I asked excitedly. That frightened/anxious feeling washed over me, and I was instantly curious. "What kind of job?"

"I figured that you would have a hard time finding something with no experience, so I pulled some strings. My dear friend Trish is the Librarian at the public library in town. She has a couple of college students who work for her, and one person just quit last week. It's not a fancy job, and it wouldn't pay much, but it's yours if you want it." Her eyebrows peaked as she waited for me to respond.

The library would be perfect for me. I mean I didn't know much about the job itself, but I loved to read. Not to mention all the quiet time. It sounded perfect. "I'll take it. It sounds like the perfect job for me."

"Yay," she bounced in her seat. "I thought so to. I will call her first thing in the morning before I leave for work and let her know. She may want to see you, but it's only about five blocks from the house. It's a nice walk."

"Perfect."

A smile was plastered to my face for the rest of the ride home.

When we got to the house I was surprised. It wasn't at all like I'd pictured. I expected the houses to practically be sitting on top of each other, but they weren't. They had yards and the brick homes were beautiful; all very similar, but older and almost historic like. I loved it.

She gave me the grand tour of the place. It was two stories, and both bedrooms were up stairs. Each room was very spacious and had its own bathroom. Nothing compared to my bedroom back home. The cream painted walls was soft and inviting. It was a lot to take in all at once, but I couldn't wait to spend some alone time in there. I sat my bag on the bed, and followed her back to the first floor.

It was so nice. There was a large kitchen that opened to a dining room, another bathroom, a large living room, and a utility room. There was even a sunroom off the back porch. I could already tell that it would be my favorite place. I could imagine myself out there with my notebook, scribbling away.

Poetry was my biggest love.

Several nights I would write to escape, and over the years my writing had just become second nature. I loved it like I loved the color green, and almost as much as I loved fried chicken. That was a whole heck of a lot. I wasn't exceptionally good at it, but I didn't mind. No one else would see it besides me anyway.

"I hope that you'll make yourself at home, and I don't ever want you to think that you can't stay here. You're welcome here as long as you want. I get pretty lonely sometimes, so it'll be nice having you around." Her voice was genuine.

"Thanks Aunt Darcy."

"Of course honey. I'm going to start supper. There are plenty of things in your room that you might need. A new toothbrush, and all your bathroom goods, and I put my old laptop in the top dresser drawer if you want to keep up with the outside world." She winked.

It sounded unusual when she said the words, "outside world." What would I know about anything or anyone outside this house? I was clueless. I would never use her laptop, but it was a nice gesture. It wasn't as if I were leaving any real friends behind besides the animals. The only friend I had back home was just an acquaintance, a stranger that I had seen only on occasion. Our parents had dinner together maybe once every few months, and she and I would hang out. We rode horses and played with the dogs. She seemed nice, and was truthfully the only person in the world I had ever considered a friend. I didn't know much about her except her name. Molly Rogers. I wouldn't even know how to contact her if I could. We had a computer at our house that was used for several things, but talking to friends wasn't one of them.

Maybe I was deprived of things in my childhood, but I never felt that way. I was never exposed to very much, so I never really knew what I was missing out on, or if I was missing anything at all. I liked it that way. The simple life suited me just fine.

Aunt Darcy pulled her apron off the hook hanging next to the pantry door, and I cringed a little at the sight of it. The ruffled edges and light pink color, reminded me of my mother. That woman would have slept in the dreadful thing if she could have. I swear she was constantly cooking or baking. She hardly ever left the kitchen. Seeing Darcy pull it over her head made my stomach knot up. I could barely look at her.

"I'm going to go and take a shower and clean up, then I'll come back and help with supper. If you want?" I said trying to rush away quickly.

"Sounds good."

I nodded and turned towards the stairs. I could hear the distant sound of her humming as I climbed the stairs fleetingly.

After the long bus ride, I was tired and stinky. Well, I couldn't really smell myself, but if I had to guess I'd say I was.

I took the stairs two at a time.

2

Jackson

For the second day in a row I was late for basketball camp. The team was hosting a day camp for the local kids, and it was mandatory for us to be there especially the starters. Coach was going to flip his lid. Playing chauffeur to my baby sister was going to cost me the starting spot on the team. The spot I'd worked too damn hard to earn. It was all going down the drain because she couldn't decide which pair of shoes she wanted to wear to work. I swear I'd love to strangle that girl sometimes.

Mom and Dad promised me that they'd make sure Kennedy's car was out of the shop this week. But when they called the mechanic he had mysteriously found five more problems under the hood. Go figure.

I see now why my older brother Tucker moved out the first chance he got. If I had a job instead of playing basketball then I'd move out too.

My cell phone dinged with a text message just as I pulled into the parking lot. I didn't have time for it. I tossed it across the seat and into my gym bag, and rushed to get inside.

Through the windows of the gym door I could see that Coach had his arms crossed over his chest with a whistle in his mouth. I burst through the door in a hurry. I didn't even bother explaining. He wouldn't have listened anyway. I ran over and joined my team along the far wall making sure that I didn't even make eye contact with him. I didn't have to see his face to know that he was staring. I could feel his eyes burning holes through the back of my shirt.

"Dude, where you been? Coach is going to slaughter you." Jeremy, one of my teammates nudged my arm.

"I had to give Kennedy a ride to work again." I bent down and tightened the laces on my shoes.

"You should have called me man. I would have given her a ride."

He was way to enthusiastic when he said ride, so I elbowed him hard in the kneecap.

"Ouch, damn."

"She's my sister." I growled, standing back up to face him.

"And she's hot." He jumped back out of arms reach so that my fists wouldn't reach him. "She's eighteen man. Get a grip."

"Drop it." My look was serious, and I meant it. He needed to keep his snide comments to himself. It's not like I was trying to get with his sister. Not that I would. She was weird, and her glasses were as thick as coke bottles. I wouldn't be caught dead with her. It'd be social suicide.

It drove me crazy when the guys talked like that about Kennedy. I knew that she was grown, and beautiful, but they didn't even try to hide their attraction. They threw it up in my face. It infuriated me to the point where I wanted to bash their faces in.

I shook it off and went to work with the kids. After all, that was why we were there in the first place. I wasn't going to stand around any longer listening to their bull crap.

The kids we were hosting at this camp were so little, barely big enough to dribble a ball. I'd been that young when I started playing, and over the years the game had it's ups and downs. Many times I wanted to just give up and quit, especially in high school. Other things seemed more important at the time, like girls. Even now they were still a distraction. But being on a scholarship meant that I couldn't afford to be distracted. Most of the guys on the team had more disturbances than they knew what to do with.

I only had one.

Holly.

She was my girlfriend of two years, and she was more than enough for me to handle. At times she was too much.

In the beginning I got with her because she was hot, and had a promising reputation. It started out as fun. The occasional lay, when I didn't want to sleep around. We were together a couple of nights a week with no strings attached. Then one day she acted all female-like and demanded that I give her more. Being with me in the bedroom wasn't enough for her. She was a good piece off ass, a real good piece of ass, so I agreed. I didn't know what I'd be getting myself into. No one told me either. I get exhausted just thinking about it.

She was everywhere, and I meant everywhere. It was real hard at first, what with the constant calling, and showing up everywhere I was. Finally after working out all the kinks, we just sort of fell into this comfortable routine. I like comfortable. If she'd just quit bitching so much it'd probably be worth the effort. Fourteen text messages a day was thirteen too many. Especially since I was trying to keep my head on straight. Basketball had to be my first priority.

My grades had dropped, and my parent's were constantly on my ass. They were nagging me everyday about this and that. Whether or not I was doing my part to keep my grades from sinking. My scholarship was on the line, so I had to keep my shit together. There was no screwing it up. It wasn't an option, and for the life of me, I couldn't make her understand. She was needy and wanting, and she knew just the right buttons to push to keep me running back when I should've been more focused.

After two hours of sweating my ass off with the kids, I just wanted to go home and relax for a little while before I had to pick Kennedy up from work. It was going to be a long night of studying for me.

I managed to get dressed, say my goodbyes, and walk out of that gym without an hour-long lecture from the coach. He wouldn't forget though. My guess was that I'd be running laps at our next practice.

After I tossed my bag into the passenger seat, I reached for my phone.

Eight messages and four missed calls flashed on the screen. I groaned at the sight of them. Every single one was from Holly.

"Where are you?" She said when she answered her phone.

"You know I had basketball camp today. We just got finished."

"Oh, well I tried to call you a couple of times. I was worried."

Yeah, right, just a couple of times. I rolled my eyes. "I'm fine. I have to go home and study some before I pick Kennedy up from work." It was times like these that I was glad I no longer had to live on campus. It helped having parents who gave generously to the college. Besides if anyone asked, there was still a room there with my name on it. Only it was being occupied with one person instead of two.

"You want me to come hang out with you tonight. I could help you study." Her voice purred into the phone. The seduction in her voice overflowed. Immediately my pants got a little tighter. She knew exactly how to catch my attention. Like I said before, she knew which buttons to push. It always worked.

"Yeah, okay. I'll call you later tonight."

"Later baby," she made a kissing sound into the phone.

I took a deep breath and tossed my phone back into the seat. Looked like I'd have to spend the rest of the week studying my ass off, instead of the rest of the night. I had plans.

It would be worth it. That girl knew how to relieve some stress.

3

Grace

Talk about nervous. First day, at my first job, and I was totally freaking out. I wore my favorite blue skirt with a white button up blouse and pulled my hair back away from my face in a long braid. Even though I was comfortable and I felt like I looked nice, it still did nothing for my nerves.

Aunt Darcy had already left for work, but she said it was safe for me to walk. I trusted her, and I didn't mind walking at all. She drove me there after supper last night so I knew exactly where it was. The walk seemed easy enough.

From the way Darcy talked, I would probably just be doing paperwork today, but I was hoping that my new boss would put me right to work. Otherwise, I'd be moping around the house with nothing to do while I waited for Darcy to get home from work.

I slipped on my favorite white shoes that I knew would be great for walking, and grabbed my shoulder bag from the dresser, draping it across my body.

Despite being nervous about the job, I really hadn't felt better. There were no crazy animal noises to wake me up at the crack of dawn, no one yelling at me to pick up my pace, and especially no dad. For once I didn't feel like I needed to tiptoe across my bedroom, although I did it anyway. Habit I guess. Somewhere deep down inside of me I felt like I just wanted to scream, or sing really loud in the shower. But, that would have to wait until later.

When I glanced at the clock I knew that I needed to start walking. I wasn't exactly sure how long it was going to take me to get there by foot, and I couldn't be late on my first day.

No way.

The morning sunlight felt warm against my cheeks when I stepped outside. It was a beautiful day. The air was much different here then it was back home. Aunt Darcy mentioned that the night air was a little cooler so I hoped my sweater would be enough until I could get something a little warmer. I'd only brought what little necessities that were most important at the time, and a coat wasn't one of them.

I made the walk in a fairly short amount of time. I didn't take the time to stop and admire the scenery because I was too excited for my first day on the job. Well, hopefully it would be my first day.

The door opened quietly at the library and there were already a few people inside reading. The smell was wonderful, and my first thought was how perfect this place was going to be for me. It was quiet and serene, everything I was.

A tall lady wearing a pair of purple-framed glasses stood behind the desk. Before I had even made the walk there, she spotted me. By the look on her face, she knew exactly who I was. Not that I didn't stick out like a sore thumb.

She moved quickly around the desk and welcomed me with open arms. That must have been the most common welcome gesture in these parts. I knew that she was Trish the Librarian from her warm welcome. She patted my back like we were old friends, and I nearly threw up on her because of my nerves. Aunt Darcy assured me of just how wonderful Trish was, and that I shouldn't worry. But I couldn't help it. It was a brand new adventure for me, a crossover into the real world.

Thankfully Darcy was right. Trish was super sweet, and she was so grateful that I was able to get started on such short notice. Her kind words made me feel much more comfortable. It only took about ten minutes to fill out my paperwork and then she put me right to work.

Trish introduced me to the other girl working on the same shift. Her name was Kennedy, and if I had to guess I'd say she and I were close in age. On the outside we were polar opposites. She wore a pair of jeans so tight that I wondered how she moved, and bright red lipstick that you could see coming from miles away. She was a very pretty girl, and probably very popular from the look of her. Her voice was loud though. That was something I wasn't used to. Of course my knowledge on the human race was mostly non-existent.

I assumed there was no dress code, seeing as everyone was wearing something different. I didn't bother asking.

Trish asked Kennedy to show me around and wanted me to shadow her for the day until I got the hang of things. It was a great idea. Kennedy really seemed to know her way around. She was so friendly too. She didn't look at me the way most people did when they first saw me. She was kind, and honestly nothing like I'd expected.

"Where are you from?" She asked as we separated the books on the cart. Her loud voice carried through the library, and I caught Trish eyeing us from over top of her glasses. Kennedy just waved it off as if it were no big deal.

"Oklahoma," I replied in a hushed tone.

"Are you going to school?"

"Eventually, I think. I'm living with my aunt right now, and my plans were just to work and save some money. At least until I get on my feet. Back home, I sort of had a sheltered life. This is my first time being away. I kind of just want to experience a little freedom. You know?" I'm not sure why I went into so much detail. I hardly knew the girl, but she seemed so easy to talk to.

Her perfect smile stretched all the way across her face. "I figured."

I snickered. "I know. I'm sure I look like such an outsider." I held out my skirt. Not that I minded.

"It's not the clothes, although I assume your entire wardrobe looks like that." She smiled sweetly. "You just have this very innocent look about you."

I wasn't sure what she meant by that, so I just shrugged my shoulders and continued stocking the shelves.

The hours passed by so fast, and I was sad to see my first day on the job end so quickly. Kennedy showed me how to close up for the day and we walked out together. Even though she was a good teacher, I figured she'd probably have to show me several more times before I fully got the hang of it.

"So I guess I'll see you tomorrow," I said slipping on my sweater. Casual conversation seemed kind of awkward to me, and I hoped that she wouldn't notice how socially dis-challenged I was. Of course, we'd been together all day and she hadn't said anything. Maybe I wasn't so bad after all.

"I have class in the morning but I'll be in for the afternoon shift." She replied.

"Okay, I'll see you then. Have a good night."

Just as we were saying our goodbyes and I started to walk away, a car sped up to the curb and honked the horn. I was worried at first until Kennedy let me know that it was her ride.

I waved at her as she walked away.

"Hey Grace," Kennedy yelled and I turned around. "Do you need a ride home?" She called out.

I heard someone yelling from inside the car. It sounded like whoever it was, was against the idea.

"I'm fine, but thank you." Besides, I didn't care much for strangers, and I didn't want to ride in the car with someone I'd never met before.

"Okay, see you tomorrow." She waved goodbye. I buttoned up my sweater and started my walk home.

Truthfully, I never expected the day to go so well. The job was much easier than I expected it'd be, and I made a friend. It was so much more than I could have ever imagined. I hoped that it was just a little taste of all of the good things to come.

4

Jackson

"Don't freaking offer someone a ride when it's not your car." I took off before Kennedy had barely shut her door.

"I was just being nice. Damn, what crawled up your ass?"

"Maybe I'd be in a better mood if someone hadn't made me late for practice."

"Seriously Jackson, we're back to this? I said I was sorry, now get over it already."

I rolled my eyes. She was such a pain in my ass sometimes.

"Who was that milk maid you were trying to give a ride to anyways?" I asked. I didn't get a good look at her face from inside the car, but those clothes were hideous. I knew I'd never seen her before. I'd remember that train wreck.

"She's the new girl, Grace. She's so nice, and really different. I like her. I think we'll be good friends."

"Whatever, she looked ridiculous. She should have hitched a ride home on her cow."

"Quit being such a dick."

"Ouch, dammit." She pinched me in the side. "It's a good thing I'm driving."

"That's what you get. Those good looks have gone straight to your head. You've turn into a superficial girl."

"You just wish you were this cool."

"Puhlease, I'm much cooler than you'll ever be, and superficial is not my color."

Sisters, I swear. Why couldn't my parent's have stopped with me?

"I cannot wait until you see Grace's face." She laughed. "I bet you'll be changing your mind real quick, because she is beautiful."

I just shook my head. I knew a beautiful girl when I saw one. She was far from it.

I opened up the stereo as loud as it would go, so I could drown out her voice.

The sooner we got home the sooner I could ditch her. One more day of riding in the same car together, and I'd probably kill her. Not literally, but damn she got on my nerves.

The television was blaring when we walked inside the house. It wasn't typical so I knew that Tucker was home. He was probably out of groceries at his house. That was his usual reason for coming home. It was never just to visit.

In the living room I found him stretched out on the couch, a sandwich was sitting on the plate that rested on his chest, and an open bag of potato chips were between his legs. He was a total mooch. Can't say I blamed him though. Mom and Dad never minded that he showed up at odd hours just to eat. Seeing him lying on the couch without a care in the world is what bothered me. Maybe I was envious.

I called out his name, but he couldn't hear me over the T.V.

"Tuck." I yelled again.

He jerked his head around to see me, but only gave me a head nod.

Figures.

free

I stomped past the couch and made my way to the kitchen. Mom and Dad weren't home or else Tucker wouldn't be slouching around like a pig. Mom would wring his neck for eating on her good sofa. I just walked in, and already he was getting on my nerves.

There was note on the refrigerator from Mom that said they wouldn't be home until late. Her and Dad had plans with the Thompson's at some fancy restaurant in town.

No wonder Tuck was here.

I scrounged through the fridge to find some leftovers and heated myself a plate. The longer I stood there watching the microwave, and listening to that damn T.V., the angrier I was getting. Tonight was so supposed to be my night to study. It was really my intention, but after arguing with Kennedy and Tucker's loud ass T.V. I just wanted to get out of the house. There was no way in hell that I was going to get any studying done now. Not here. Not in this house. The damn T.V. was too loud; I wouldn't be able to hear myself think.

Fuck it.

I'd go out instead.

I left the plate in the microwave, grabbed my keys and my books, and stormed out. I didn't even bother telling anyone I was leaving.

Before I reached the car I had already dialed Holly, and the phone was ringing.

"Hey Babe," she answered.

"Hey. I had to get out of the house. Can I come to your place?"

"Of course. Get your ass over here. I miss you."

All I heard was, – I need sex, come fuck me now. She didn't have to ask me twice.

"I'm on my way."

So much for studying, unless you counted the way my hands would be studying her body. In that case, I'm sure I'd get an A. The female anatomy was my best subject.

i am *free*

5

Grace

"I got a call from your Dad today." Aunt Darcy was giving me her saddest and most pitiful face ever.

"What did you say?" I asked. My pencil stopped tapping on my notebook as I waited for a response.

"I lied through my teeth. I told him I hadn't seen you. I sounded really worried, so I think he bought it."

I let on an exasperated breath, and hoped she was right. Things were going so great. I didn't want him messing everything up.

"You know if you want to talk about anything with me, you can." She said as she took the seat next to me on the couch.

"I know, but there's really not that much to say. You've met him." I smiled.

"Unfortunately yes."

"Exactly, I'm not ready to revisit those moments just yet."

She patted my forearm. "I understand. I really do." I could tell that she was sincere. I knew that she would be there for me no matter what. "Let's talk about something that's not so depressing. Tell me all about your first day on the job."

I started to speak, but she stopped me. That was one thing I had already learned about Aunt Darcy. Her mind raced a million miles a minute, and sometimes it was hard for me to keep up.

"Tell me in the kitchen. I need to make us some dinner." She waved me into the kitchen, and I followed.

I slid my bare feet across her floor so that I could feel the softness between my toes as I made my way towards the kitchen. The carpet on her floor was a nice change from what I was used to. It was warm and inviting. I actually walked around barefoot all the time here. Not like at home. At home you'd get splinters from the old hard wood floors.

"So, did you have a good day? Were they nice to you?" She asked.

"It was great. The job wasn't too hard, and I caught on really quick. The computer is still a bit tricky, but I think I'll get the hang of it."

"You will." She said.

"I think I even made a friend, a young girl about my age. Her name is Kennedy, and boy was she different. She was so nice though, and very pretty."

Darcy turned around and gave me a quizzical look. I knew she'd be surprised.

"Look at you," she smiled big. "I'm proud of you. You are so young and you should be making friends, and living life. This change of pace is going to be good for you. I can already see it."

"You think?" I propped my elbows up on the counter and rested my head in my hands.

"Oh honey, I know." She kissed my cheek. "Oh, I forgot to mention that Paul is going to come over for dinner. I can't wait for you to meet him."

"Paul?"

Her face lit up when she spoke his name. I didn't need to ask anymore. She loved this Paul guy. I could see it all over her face. Just saying his name made her all flustered.

"He's so great. You're going to love him, and he can't wait to meet you too."

The glow radiated from her skin. If she loved him this much, how could I not?

"I'll go wash up a bit, and change clothes. Then I'll be back down to help anyway I can."

She shooed me away, and I hurried upstairs. I was actually thrilled. We were having a dinner party. It wasn't something that I was used to. It was exciting and new. It made me giddy like a child. I hoped I wouldn't make a complete fool of myself.

I dressed in my Sunday best. It was the nicest skirt I owned. It was crème colored and had very tiny lace work around the seams. Glancing at myself in the mirror, I smiled. I cleaned up nice.

Darcy gave me her seal of approval when I walked back into the kitchen.

"Will you set the table? Everything you need is in the china cabinet." She pointed to the massive wooden cabinet against the far wall. "Oh, can you keep an eye on the food while I go change. He should be here any minute."

"Sure." I giggled at her. She was hopping around all frantic like. It was funny to watch. I wondered to myself if all people that were truly in love acted like that. My parents never did.

As I placed the last setting at the table the doorbell rang.

"Grace, can you get that. I'm in my underwear."

I laughed. There was never a dull moment with that woman. Then for a brief moment my face fell. I had this mental image of Darcy cantering out wearing nothing but her underwear. Hopefully that wasn't going to be a sight that I needed to get used to seeing. I shook off the thought.

I peeked out the side window near the door and saw a man standing there. He was holding flowers –very sweet, and I knew that it had to be Paul. I didn't make him wait any longer. Opening the door, I found him standing there with a big smile on his face.

"Hello," I said.

"You must be Grace." His voice was deep, and there was a cute little dimple on his cheek. I nearly blushed. Handsome man and conversation, my social skills were about to work overtime. I looked down at my feet, but I couldn't keep the smile off my face. He was older, clearly older than Darcy, but I could see her interest. He was a very good-looking man.

"It's nice to meet you. Paul right?" I fumbled with my words a bit.

"That's me."

I stood back and let the door open wider. "Come in?"

"Thank you. These are for you." He held the flowers out to me.

"For me?" I was shocked. I hadn't ever gotten flowers before, and I was surprised that he'd brought them for me and not Darcy.

"Darcy told me that you were family. Like a daughter to her." He leaned in a little closer and whispered, "I was trying to make a good impression."

I couldn't help the laugh that escaped. "Great job. Your secret is safe with me." I said, in return.

He already won me over, and I'd only just met him. I understood easily why Darcy was head over heels for him.

"Something smells great," he said slipping out of his coat.

"Oh food! Excuse me." I rushed into the kitchen. I could hear Paul snickering behind me.

Luckily nothing was burned.

Paul took a chair at the table while I rushed around.

"Do you have any kids?" I asked him. I was trying not to be too forward, though he didn't seem to mind. I was just making conversation.

"Yes and no." He answered.

I eyed him curiously, unsure of what he meant.

"I don't have any of my own," He said. "But I have a stepdaughter. My ex wife had a child from a previous marriage and I raised her from the time she was about five years old. She's my daughter. I still see her all the time, even though she's grown now."

"That's really great of you. What's her name?"

"Carly," he smiled when he said her name.

"Paul," Darcy said as she walked backed into the room. Her face lit up, and so did his. Together, they made a handsome couple. They seemed perfect for each other.

"Hey babe," he pulled her into a hug and they shared a kiss that made my face light up like Rudolph's nose.

Whoa! I had to turn away.

"I heard you talking about Carly. Grace, I can't wait for you to meet her. She's a wonderful girl, only a couple of years older than you."

"That sounds great, I'd love to meet her."

Darcy and I carried the food over to the table. She'd really outdone herself with all of this food. I was under the impression that she couldn't cook like this, but that wasn't the case. She just didn't like to cook for just herself, and I could understand that.

We had such a great dinner. The three of us talked and laughed. I had never had such a carefree meal in all of my life. There were no unseen eggshells that we had to tiptoe around. There was no worry of saying something that may make someone else angry. It was light conversation and it felt normal, and real.

I told Darcy that I'd clean up the kitchen so that the two of them could take a walk. Walk was code for more kissing I was sure.

Cleaning up was the least I could do.

There was a dishwasher under the cabinet, but I opted not to use it. Hand washing dishes was the only thing I'd ever learned to do. We never had one of those fancy things at home. Manual labor was all I'd ever learned. My Dad wouldn't dare spend the money for something that his wife and child could manually do. It'd be a waste of money.

Suddenly the thought of home had my mind lingering on what they were doing. I wondered mostly about my mother. Sure she probably wasn't thinking about me, but I couldn't help but think about her. Believe it or not, there were a couple of good things about her. Those memories were all in my childhood, but at least I still had them.

I continued with the dishes hoping that those thoughts would just leave. Any time spent thinking about them, was time wasted as far as I was concerned. I couldn't worry about that now. My new life was just beginning, and I didn't want to dwell on the past.

After I finished the dishes I went upstairs to write for a bit. My notebook of poetry entries had become like a diary for me. I wrote something inside of it everyday. Mostly about my day-to-day life, or things that had stuck out to me. No matter how plain or ordinary, I still wrote.

It was my escape.

It's funny how time flies when you're happy, and how it moves slowly like a snail when you're not. Already I had done a whole bunch things since my time here. I could write about so many wonderful things, but what stood out most to me was my new friendship. I couldn't believe how easy it was for me to relate to someone. Just to share conversation with someone my age. Kennedy was so different, but in a good way. I was thankful for a friend. So, that was what I wanted to write about.

Today, A Good Day

Eighteen years is a long time, to never have a friend.

To never talk, to never laugh, to never lend a helping hand.

I met her today; she was warm and kind.

Befriending me without thinking, her eyes were not blind.

Despite our differences, she talked all day.

Friendly conversations, but more work than play.

Who would have guessed that me, with so little to say.

Would make a friend.

A FRIEND!

Today, was a good day.

I closed my notebook. The words were simple, but perfect. I couldn't wait to get back to work. Tomorrow would be a new day, and hopefully just as great.

6

Jackson

The morning came too damn fast. I didn't get home from Holly's until after midnight and I got zero studying done.

Perfect.

Classes started in thirty minutes and I had nothing complete. Not only was the coach going to kill me, but my parents were too. My grades were slipping. I had to study tonight. No more excuses. Holly was just going to have to understand, and I knew that wouldn't be an easy conversation.

I stood at the bottom of the stairs screaming at Kennedy to get her ass in gear. She wasn't going to make me late today. If she didn't come down in the next five minutes, I'd just leave her home.

"The clock is ticking. Let's go. Now!" I screamed.

"I'm coming. Get your panties out of a knot." She hopped down the stairs. She was way too chipper for so early in the morning, and already getting on my last nerve.

I growled and clenched my fist at my side. Shaking my head I stormed out the door. She'd better run was all I had to say.

She barely made it inside my car before I took off, and the first five minutes of our drive was a bitch fest. Slow down, you're an ass, grow up, the list was endless. I couldn't say what I wanted to say back to her, because she'd run back and tell Mom like we were five years old. She was the baby of the family, and she got away with everything. Not me. It didn't matter that I was an adult. As long as I was living under my parent's roof, I still had rules.

I let her continue to rant and tried to tune her out. Thank goodness school wasn't that far away. It was normally about a fifteen-minute drive, but that day I made it in ten.

Kennedy hurried off to meet her friends as soon as I parked. I tossed up deuces at her back, thanking God that I didn't have to spend the rest of my day with her. Sure, I loved my sister. Like, I wouldn't let anyone hurt her or anything. But that was my job. I didn't have to like her, and at that moment... I didn't.

"Hey man. You had a good night didn't you?" Jeremy caught up to me as I walked inside.

"It wasn't bad. Looks like Holly's been running her chops this morning." I glanced back at him.

"She told Lacey, Lacey told Amber. The list goes on and on." He smiled big.

"Dude, you sound like a chick right now. You may need to get your balls fitted for a sequined sack."

"Shut up." He pushed open the doors with a little force.

"Shut up," I laughed. "That's the best you got." I punched his arm.

He rolled his eyes. "I got get to class. Are you still going to The Edge this weekend? I think everybody's in." He asked. The Edge- a local club where all of the cool kids hung out. Better known as the place to get lit up and party until two a.m.

"I don't know man. If I don't get some studying done, I'm not going anywhere."

"How far behind are you?"

"Too far." I admitted.

"I had to get a tutor, maybe you need one too. Coach hooked me up. I know he'll help you to. Don't stress. The weekend is still four days away."

"We'll see. I got to go." I said backing in the direction of my class.

"I'll catch you later." He called out.

I nodded my head at him.

My literature class was the usual bore. Our essay papers were due, and mine was not finished. I was far from it. I don't know if it was my lucky day or what. Mr. Colby was out for some reason and the lady sitting in for his class told us that he was giving us a two-day extension on our papers. Two days. Hell yes. An outline was the only thing I had done, and it wasn't that great.

It was time for me to get to work. Seriously. I couldn't slack anymore.

My next two classes seemed to fly by. Of course I was behind in both of those too. It was going to be a long night at the library for me.

I sent Holly a text telling her that I couldn't see her or talk to her tonight. I didn't wait for her whiny reply. She'd try to convince me otherwise, and dammit she could do it. She had way too much power over me, way too much.

Kennedy was at the car waiting when I walked out. That was a first. Normally, I'd have to hunt her down.

"Are you taking me to work?" She asked.

"Yeah. I have some studying to do. So I need to go anyway. Get in."

We made the short drive to the library and I was stuck listening to Kennedy complain about some guy in her class. She was so obnoxious, but for some reason I couldn't stop listening today. This guy had given her trouble once before. Even though I couldn't stand her, I didn't like anyone else messing with her. I'd hate to have to beat some punk ass up.

I told her to let me know if it got worse, that I'd take care of it.

I locked my doors, and left my phone in the car to keep from getting any distractions. Mainly Holly.

My bag was heavy and I knew there was no way I'd get everything done tonight. I'd be lucky if I finished it all within the week.

I followed Kennedy inside, and found a table in the back. I didn't have to worry about her annoying me. She liked me about as much as I liked her.

The place was pretty much empty. The way I liked it. Glancing at the clock on the wall, I realized that I had four hours to get something done. That was it.

The time seemed to pass by faster than I would have liked. I barely looked up from my books. It was after dark outside. The light was no longer shining in through the window. I finished the rough draft of my Lit paper and one assignment for my Biology class, but I was still only half done. It looked like the library was going to be my new hangout for the week.

"Only twenty more minutes until closing Jack." Kennedy whispered.

I glanced up at her. "I just have three more questions on this sheet, and I'll be done. I can walk out with you when you close."

"All right. Hurry up."

Shit. Her snide comment made me want to jab my pencil into her hand. Tell me to hurry up. That was the pot calling the kettle black.

I had all of my papers in my bag and was making my way up front. Kennedy wasn't alone behind the desk. Little Bo Peep was with her.

"I almost forgot. My bag is in the back. You go ahead Kennedy. I have my key." The girl called out over her shoulder.

"We'll wait." Kennedy called after her.

I growled under my breath.

Only a minute later she came running from the back. "Thanks for waiting." She said. She stepped closer to us. Kennedy and I were standing at the door waiting.

My jaw dropped to the ground. Little Bo Peep was not what I expected, not at all. She was anything but. Her green eyes were big, almost too big for her face. Her skin was pale white, and her lips were… Damn those lips.

I'll be damned. This girl was beautiful, just like Kennedy said.

I snapped back into the moment when someone cleared her throat. When I flicked my eyes up to meet Kennedy's she was silently laughing at me.

What could I say?

She was right about this. Despite this girl's ridiculous clothing, she was gorgeous.

More than that even. She was an angel.

"I'm Grace," she said in a low and sweet voice. "I don't think we've met." Her eyes flicked to my face then back down. She clearly was a shy girl.

"No, I would have remembered you." I held out my hand and waited for hers. She seemed kind of stunned by my admission, but I wasn't one to hold my tongue. It's a good thing I didn't say what I was really thinking, -like damn girl.

She placed her tiny hand inside mine, and gently squeezed. Was she afraid of me? Her hand jerked free almost as quickly as it touched me.

"I'm Jackson."

She looked at me briefly than anywhere else she could find. She was avoiding eye contact. To be so beautiful, she sure was withdrawn.

"Don't mind my brother," Kennedy said as the two of them walked out of the door first. I still stood there a little shell-shocked. I had never seen a girl that looked so beautiful, and she wasn't wearing a single drop of makeup. I didn't even know that that was humanly possible. I can't tell you how many times I've went to bed with a girl and woke up with a totally different one. I laughed at the thought.

Following them outside, I waited for Kennedy to lock up. Grace had her back to me, and I was obviously checking her out. You couldn't tell much about her body, other than she was small. Her long milkmaid skirt covered everything up, and those shoes. Yikes. I didn't even know they made those canvas type shoes anymore. They were ugly. I could only imagine the way this girl got picked on.

Even I was calling her names.

"Can we give you a ride home?" I asked.

I didn't care that Kennedy was about two breaths from full on laughter.

"No thank you," she answered politely. "I don't mind the walk. It's not far."

"It's too damn cold," and it was. She was only wearing a sweater. "I'll take you."

Her eyes grew big. "Honestly, I'm fine."

"Well here then," I shrugged out of my coat. She at least was going to stay warm. I held out the coat and waited for her to put it on.

"Oh dear brother, I don't believe I've ever seen this side you before." Kennedy joked.

It didn't go unnoticed by Grace either. I could see the smile creeping up on her cheeks. She was hesitant.

"Just take it," I snapped.

She slid her tiny arms inside, and wrapped the jacket tightly around her. "Thank you." She said. "I better go."

"See you tomorrow." Kennedy said.

"Yeah, see you tomorrow. Thank you for the coat Jackson."

"You're welcome. See you tomorrow." Her head leaned to the side a little, and I smiled big. Bet she didn't know that she'd be seeing a lot more of me.

When I got inside the car, I looked in my mirror and watched that girl walk off in the opposite direction. I couldn't keep my eyes off her. Who was she, and where did she come from?

"I knew it. I knew it. I knew the moment that you laid eyes on that girl, that you'd be biting your tongue." Kennedy laughed as she buckled her seat belt.

I rolled my eyes. "Okay, so she's beautiful. I'll admit it. What's with that damn skirt though, and did you see her shoes?"

"Don't be such a superficial prick Jack. She's different. So what?"

"I'm not superficial, I'm honest. She needs some new clothes."

"Maybe she doesn't want new clothes," was Kennedy's reply. "Maybe she likes what she's wearing. She's from Oklahoma. Maybe that's what all the girl's in Oklahoma wear."

"Hell no. Colleen Marie would never be caught dead looking like that, so your theory is wrong."

"Who the hell is Colleen Marie?"

"Playboy's playmate of the month, August 2003."

"You're seriously disturbed brother. That fact that you know that is ridiculous. You were not looking at Playboy's in 2003." She huffed.

"You can search anything you want on the Internet, and that's not the point. She looks like she's part of some Little House on the Prairie farm."

"Just give it up, would you? It's not like you have a chance with her anyway. She is far too inexperienced for you."

"That can be changed." I grinned at the thought.

"Shut your face. You're getting on my nerves."

"Well it's my car and if you don't like what I have to say, then you're welcome to walk."

Thankfully, that shut her up.

I thought about Grace the rest of the ride home. I knew Kennedy was right about her being inexperienced, and I knew that truthfully I'd never have a chance, but I couldn't seem to get her out of my head. From a reputation stand point, I knew that people would chew me up and spit me out over this one, but dammit she was hot. Well, her face was, her clothes not so much. But I already had a hot girl right at my disposal. Holly was giving it up anytime I wanted it. No need chasing after something that wouldn't amount to nothing. That'd be too much work.

7

Grace

"So whose jacket are you wearing?" Aunt Darcy asked as soon as I walked in. Her eyes were bright and the smile was much too big for her face.

I hadn't even thought about her seeing me in it. I couldn't wrap my head around it myself. I'd never been around boys much, outside of my brother. It was different, and nice. Yeah, nice was a good word. Of course, I got really nervous and didn't say much, but what could he expect from me. He saw what I looked like for goodness sakes. He couldn't expect much. The entire walk home I kept thinking about how forthcoming he was. He wasn't afraid to say anything, much like his sister. But the gesture of his jacket was nice. It kept me warm the entire walk home, and it smelled so good.

"It belongs to a boy named Jackson. He is Kennedy's brother. She's the girl I was telling you about that's my friend at work. They offered me a ride home, and when I didn't except, he gave me his coat." I tried hard not to smile, but the cheesiest grin spread across my face. I knew it was cheesy, because she was all but laughing right in my face.

She was curled up on the couch with her coffee mug, and patted the spot next to her for me to sit. "So, what does he look like? Tell me all about him?"

I sat down, but I didn't want to say anything at first. You just weren't supposed to talk about these things, or maybe you were and I'd just been doing it all wrong all of these years. But whom was I supposed to talk to, certainly not my mother. And this was the hottest boy that I'd ever spoke to. Besides, he was the only boy I'd ever spoken to.

I couldn't contain myself any longer. "Oh Darcy, you should have seen him. He's so handsome. He has this dark brown hair, that is almost black, and it was fixed perfectly. I'm not sure what he uses on it, but it never moves." She laughed and I continued. "He's really tall too. Well, you can tell by this jacket, and he says whatever he's thinking. Like, he doesn't care what comes out of his mouth. I've never met anyone like him."

"Sounds like someone has a crush."

"No, I mean I don't think so. I've never really had a crush before. Besides, I don't know anything about the boy except for what he looks like, and he is way different than I am. I just met him today. Are boys always so weird?" I asked.

"Honey, you have no idea. I'm still trying to figure them out." She sighed.

"Well there is no need to worry about me. I don't suspect any boys will be looking at me with love in their eyes." I laughed at the thought. "No one will see past my clothes. I saw how he looked at me."

"Grace," she took my hand. "You have to know that you are a beautiful girl, and that the boys will most certainly be looking at you. They we will be falling for you in no time."

"No." I shook my head vigorously.

"Yes," She stated. "Does the clothes that you wear bother you? I mean you've worn them your whole life. Do you want to change?"

No one had ever asked me that before. I'd never had the option to change.

"To be honest, I don't mind the way I look. I like it. It's what I've known my whole life, and I don't want to change." It would probably make me feel like an imposter. Of course I didn't want to change.

"Good, because you don't have to. That's the beauty of it. You can dress anyway you want. If this is what you like, and what's comfortable to you, then so be it. Don't let anyone try to change you."

"I wouldn't dream of it. I don't mind not fitting in. I don't mind being different. I've known I was different my whole life. The only thing I ever wanted to change was living with my father, and I'm here now. I couldn't be happier."

She squeezed my hand. "Good, because I don't want you anywhere else. Tell me more about this boy."

"Well," I giggled. "He's got really light eyes, almost see through. I didn't look at them long because I got all flustered and shy."

"He sounds cute. I should probably warn you that boys can be very charming when they need to be. They could charm the pants right off of you, or skirt."

"Aunt Darcy, please." I slammed my hand over my face. "Can we not have this talk? I assure you that I've already talked about human reproduction with my mother."

"That's great, but she's never met the boys that are walking around here in the real world. I just want you to be prepared."

"Thank you. Let's cross that bridge if we ever get to it. We only introduced ourselves. He probably doesn't even remember my name."

Her hearty laugh filled the room. "I'd bet my paycheck that he hasn't forgotten your name."

What did that mean? Was he thinking about me? I highly doubted that. It was funny to hear myself talk about him though. I guess maybe I did have a crush on this boy that I barely knew.

It was harmless, and bound to happen sooner or later.

"Want to go out to eat for supper tonight?" She asked.

"That sounds fun. Let's do it."

"Maybe we could go to the movies too."

"Really, we can?" I nearly bounced off the couch in excitement.

"For sure. Girl's night out is happening. Go get ready."

She didn't have to ask me twice. I brushed out my hair, put on my grey sweater, and changed into my only other pair of shoes. I was ready.

Dinner was great. At least what I tasted of it. I ate so fast that I nearly made myself sick. I was excited to get to the movies.

We were in line to get popcorn when I heard someone call my name.

Both Darcy and I turned around.

"Kennedy." I smiled. "What are you doing?"

"Duh Grace. This is a movie theatre." She joked.

I smiled big. "Right of course."

The group of girls with her were staring me down. I shifted a bit on my feet at the sight of them too. "These are my friends Amanda, Kate, and Madison." Kennedy said, introducing the girls.

"Nice to meet you." I replied.

Not one of those girls said hello to me. They eyed me as though I had two heads. I guess they'd never seen anyone that looked like me. I couldn't believe that though. I was just plain; it wasn't like I had purple hair and facial piercings. Oh well.

Kennedy continued to smile as I introduced her to Aunt Darcy. She was much different than her friends. She never looked at me any differently. She was kind and spoke to Aunt Darcy as if she hadn't just met her.

"Enjoy your movie." I said to Kennedy as we took our popcorn and walked away.

"See you tomorrow at work."

"Right, see ya." I called back. She really was a nice a girl. I loved working with her. It felt so good that she'd made an effort to talk to me. We truly were friends.

"She seemed nice." Darcy said, as we took our seats in the back of the room. This wasn't the first time I'd been to the movies, but it was the first time I'd seen anything that wasn't a musical. That was all that we were allowed to see at home, and they were rare. We maybe went once my whole life.

"She really is." I didn't say anything else.

"I'm sorry those other girl's were such bitches." She said.

I shook my head and smiled. "It's nothing I haven't seen before. I don't mind. I know I'm not like them, and I'm okay with that. They're the ones with the problem, not me." I stuffed my mouth full of popcorn, as full as I could get it.

"You are a special girl, you know that? I am so proud of you. Not many girls your age would let something like that roll off their shoulders."

"When you're used to standing out, then fitting in is nonsensical."

"Always remember that Grace." Aunt Darcy had a serious look in her eyes. "Fitting in is overrated."

I smiled at her and settled back in my chair. I would. I was born to stand out, and I didn't intend to change for anyone. I loved myself.

No one would change me.

No one.

8

Jackson

Sleeping was for the dead, I supposed. It sure as hell wasn't for me. I stayed up late to try and finish more class work, but wound up with one thing on my mind. Or one girl I should say.

It had been a long time since I'd let one person occupy that much of my time. I couldn't escape her. She was unusually different. So much so, that I wanted to laugh at her one moment, and bend her over that librarian desk the other.

Gah. Why couldn't I get her off my mind?

For the first time in a while, I was the one running late. Nothing was working right. My one-track mind was on the wrong path. I couldn't get anything to work this morning, and it was pissing me off. It was almost like having two left feet and hands that didn't work.

Kennedy screamed at me twice to get my ass in gear.

"I'm coming." I growled.

I needed an energy drink bad.

Mom told me last night that Kennedy's car still wasn't ready. Of course it wasn't. I was stuck with her at least for the next two days. JOY!

"Should I drive?" She eyed me curiously.

"Hell no." I pushed past her, out the door.

"Your shirt is on inside out." She yelled.

"SHIT!" I tossed my bag in the back of the car. I rolled the shirt off my back and fixed it quickly. "Get in the car."

"What's with you today?" Kennedy asked.

"I just didn't get much sleep. That's all."

"Maybe you should quit spending so much of your night time hours with Holly. That might help."

"Maybe you should mind your own business," I slammed the door closed. "Besides my lack of sleep has nothing to do with Holly."

"Right."

"Yeah. Right." I put the car in reverse. "I'm in a mood, can we just have some silence this morning please?" I ran my fingers through my hair.

"My pleasure." She replied.

I only had one class today, and then an afternoon weight session with the guys. Off-season training was sometimes more exhausting then regular practices, especially when I was running on three hours of sleep.

I could barely stay awake in class. My eyes were so heavy, and I don't think I heard a single word that the professor said. Lucky for me Holly was in this class too. She was the note taker. I could get everything I needed from her.

"Why are you so tired to day?"

I placed my hand on the small of her back and helped her walk a little faster out of the room. "I told you earlier that I didn't get much sleep."

"Why?" She asked, as she dug around her suitcase of a purse.

"I had a paper that needed to be finished, and I'm still not done." I didn't have the energy to argue with her. Not today.

"Okay, well, am I gonna get to see you later tonight?"

"I doubt it babe," I added a little extra sugar so that she wouldn't aggravate the hell out of me. "After weights

I'm going back to the library to try and finish my paper. I won't be home until late."

Her bottom lip stuck out, and made me chuckle. "Stop that. We're going out this weekend."

"Fine, but I'll miss you."

"Mmm… How much?" I leaned down and kissed her lips lightly.

She wrapped her arms around my neck and deepened the kiss. "A lot." She nipped my bottom lip.

For one whole minute, I almost forgot that I had a ton of things to do. Almost. That was the effect she had on me.

"I got to go babe."

"Okay, but call me later."

"I will." I waved bye and watched as she walked away. Her tight little ass swayed back and forth with each step. She had the cutest butt. I loved watching her walk away. There was much pleasure in the curve of a woman's back where it met her plump ass, an irresistible pleasure.

I had to shake off the dirty thoughts to keep myself from sporting a boner in front of the guys.

When she walked through the double door and out of my sight, I ran off to the weight room. I was fifteen minutes early. There was no way I was going to give the

74

coach any reason to be pissed off again. He could be brutal.

"My sweaty ass balls are glued to the side of my leg," Worm yelled out from the bench next to mine. "I'm hitting the showers."

"Seriously man," I huffed out a large breath while lifting the bar high above my head. "I didn't need to know that." A soft laugh escaped me.

"Just keeping it real." He called out tossing his sweaty rag in my direction.

"You're going to The Edge this weekend right?" Jeremy asked. He stood behind me and helped me place the bar back in place.

I sat up and wiped the sweat from my face. "I told you I don't know yet. Probably, but I have to see how much work I get done today and tomorrow. I don't need more reasons to fall behind."

"You'll be fine." He insisted. He always insisted. He could be as needy as Holly sometimes.

I rolled my eyes and stood up from the bench. I let out an exasperated breath as I walked over to where the barbells were lined against the wall. Grabbing my choice of weight, I sat down on the bench close by. Slowly I curled the weight up to my chest.

"Coach isn't even in here. Why are you still lifting?" Jeremy made his way over next to me.

"Some of us still do as we're told you know? We can't all be so perfect on the court and slack off." I retorted.

"Psh." He smirked. "Whatever, I'm going to take a shower. You better come this weekend."

Nodding my head I replied, "You know I'll probably be there."

My response sufficed him. It didn't take much to twist my arm. He knew I'd come. That's probably why my grades were for shit. Too many times I'd went to The Edge or someone's house party or even spent the night cozied up in the bed with Holly.

Grades didn't come easy to me. I always had to work hard to rake by, but add slacking off on top of it and it made for a disaster. Now I'd have to spend the rest of the semester digging myself out of the hole I'd buried myself in.

"Quitting time Jack." The coach called out to me as he walked back into the weight room from his office. I was the only one left in the room and he waved his clipboard around so that I'd notice I was alone.

"Got it coach."

I placed the weights back against the wall and rushed off to the showers. No one else was in there thankfully, because I wasn't in the mood to listen to there bullshit. I wanted to hurry and finish and get my ass to the library.

Rubbing my hands hard against my scalp I let the warm water rush down over me and rinse away the shampoo.

My record timing shower had me at the library only fifteen minutes after weights was over. The door opened easily, and as I walked inside I immediately scanned the desk for Grace. I knew that she'd be there somewhere. However, I didn't see her as I walked in and found a table close to the back and beside the window. The seclusion was always nice. I needed complete silence to work. My brain wouldn't function otherwise.

A couple of times I looked up from my notebook in search of the girl that I couldn't keep my mind off of. I never saw her though. Maybe she hadn't come into work after all. I buried myself deeper into my books and tried to pound out some work. She'd just be a distraction anyway.

I don't know how long I sat there, but I was aware that I had read the last paragraph three times and still had no clue what it said. My eyelids were too heavy and I'd started to lose focus.

"Jackson." I heard a soft voice call out my name.

When I looked up I saw Grace standing there across from my table. Her head tilted slightly to the side and her blonde braid laid flat against the front of her shirt. I started to speak, but I guess I'd been staring too long. She spoke instead.

"I brought your jacket back. I wasn't sure if you would be here." She hesitated. "It's behind the desk up front."

"Oh right, my jacket." I smiled up at her and watched as she shifted her gaze to the floor, and I couldn't help but smile bigger. She was so shy. "You can keep it if you need it."

"That's okay. I'm fine." She replied.

She took a step back, and I knew that she was about to walk away. I quickly spoke again hoping to keep her there a little longer.

"Hey, do you know anything about college Lit?"

She shook her head and pressed her lips together tightly. "I don't know. I've never taken any college courses."

I sat my pencil down on the notebook in front of me, and leaned back in my chair. "I'm supposed to write a paper on one of the books on the professor's list. We had to randomly choose them out of a bucket he passed around the room."

"That sounds exciting." Her eyes lit up. "Which book did you choose?"

I held up the paperback and glared at her.

I could tell she was fighting back laughter. "I'm sorry." She tried to keep a straight face. "You just don't strike me as a Jane Eyre kind of guy."

I sat there for a minute keeping a stern look on my face, but I couldn't hold it in any longer. I had to laugh too, because she was right. Just her face alone was making me it hard for me to keep my composure.

"I'm sorry." She apologized again.

"No, I don't mind. It was funny. You were funny." I said. "So have you read Jane Eyre, because you do seem like that kind of girl"?

"I have." She nodded.

I knew it. "Good, sit down."

"I can't. I have to get back to work." She pointed over her shoulder.

"It'll be okay. I just need someone to read what I've written. I have to have a second opinion. My grades are depending on it." I pouted my lip hoping to sway her decision.

She looked over her shoulder, and then towards me. "Okay." She held out her hand.

I handed her my paper, and leaned back and watched her as she read.

She hadn't even made it through the first page when she sat the paper back down on the table.

"What's wrong?" I asked.

"Uh," she hesitated.

"Just say it."

"You haven't read the book." She blurted out.

"Yes I have," I lied.

"Nope." She shook her head.

"Okay fine. So I skimmed it. Not a big deal."

"You have to read the book."

I growled under my breath. "I don't have enough time now to read the book, and I need a good grade."

"Well, I'm no literature professor, but he or she will know you didn't read it. Your information is all wrong."

"SHIT!" I called out a little too loud.

Grace flinched at my words and took a jolting step back.

"I'm sorry, I just," I paused for a moment and ran my hands through my hair. "My grades are all ready in the tank and I needed to get a decent grade on this paper. My basketball scholarship is on the line."

I'd fucking read the book if I had the time, but I don't, and now I'm screwed.

"Um," Grace started to speak and I looked up to see a sympathetic look on her face. "I can help you if you'd like."

She was serious. I could tell. She wouldn't lie. Girl's like her didn't lie.

"You'd do that?"

She shook her head yes, and stepped closer to the table. "We're closing in about an hour, so I could help you tomorrow if you want. I don't have to work tomorrow."

"It's due tomorrow," I interjected.

Her cute little nose scrunched up tight when she said, "Well shoot."

I had to laugh at her. Her words were adorable and delicate just like her.

"Just say it. I want to hear you say it." I laughed.

"Say what," she said.

"Shit." I smiled big. "Come on little Gracie." I teased. "Say it."

She rolled her eyes. "What? You think I can't say it."

"Nope. You're innocent little mouth has never said those words."

She shook her head. "You have no idea what my mouth has said," and her eyes grew big at her confession. It was as if she couldn't believe she'd said it.

"What are you guys talking about?" Kennedy said.

"I'm just corrupting your girl here." I admitted.

"Don't listen to a single word that comes out of his mouth. He's filled with useless information and shit."

Grace smiled.

"Grace here has kindly agreed to help me finish my paper for my lit class."

"Oh really." Her voice was exaggerated.

"I don't know when I'll have the time." Grace said. "Didn't you say it was due tomorrow?"

"Yeah, but I can come over to your place after you get off work tonight."

"Uh."

I thought about the words and realized that she'd probably be uncomfortable. Maybe I pushed her too quick.

"Unless you have plans. In that case I'll just be up until sunrise, no big deal." I let the guilt settle in.

She let out a sigh. "Let me just call my aunt and make sure she doesn't mind."

Yes! She was easily persuaded. I didn't even have to stick out my lip. It was my chance to be alone with her, even if all we were doing was studying. Plus, I was going to ace this paper for Lit class.

"Be right back." She called over her shoulder as she walked off.

I watched her as she walked away. I wished her skirt had been a little tighter so I could see a hint of what her body looked like. There was no way of knowing with that garbage sack she was wearing.

Kennedy leaned across the table and in a hushed but aggravated tone she said, "What the hell are you doing?"

"Getting some much needed help with this paper."

"Bullshit. I know your intentions involve more than studying."

"I'm not going to deflower her. I'm going to get an A on this damn paper, and I'm going to stare at her while I do it."

"God you're such a douche Jackson. She's an innocent girl who doesn't need your kind trying to persuade her otherwise." Her jaw was clinched and there was an evil look in her eyes.

"I'm glad you think so little of me. Damn Kennedy. I know she's different. I'm not going to cross any lines with her, so please just shut the fuck up about it. I really have to pass this class. My scholarship is on the line. She's willing to help and I'm taking it. Even if I did have to twist her arm to do it." I said in anger.

I could see her facial expression ease up. "Well," she faltered. "Just don't do anything stupid."

"I won't. I have a girlfriend."

"Yeah. Right. Girlfriend." She rolled her eyes as she walked away.

She really thinks so little of me, and I guess she has good reason. But it pisses me off. I wouldn't mess with some innocent girl just to get my kicks. This paper meant basketball or no basketball.

9

Grace

"What was I thinking?" I whispered to myself as I walked up to the phone behind the desk. A boy. Coming to my house. One little pouty whine and I agreed, like and idiot. I liked to help people, and I felt so sorry for him. His pitiful story about his scholarship sucked me right in. But what if he was lying? Would he lie to me? I mean I didn't even know him. I didn't know what his intentions were or if he was telling me the truth.

"Stop it." I quietly said to myself. He's Kennedy's brother. It would be harmless. He really needed my help.

I picked up the phone and dialed the number to Aunt Darcy's cell. She answered on the first ring.

"Hello." She said.

"Aunt Darcy."

"Hey Grace. Is everything okay."

"Uh, yeah." I paused for a minute. "Do you remember me telling you about Kennedy's brother Jackson. He was the guy whose coat I wore home yesterday."

"Of course. The crush."

I could hear her smiling on the other end of the line.

"Yep, that's the one."

"What about him?" She asked.

"He has a paper that's due tomorrow that he needs help on. I kind of told him that I would help, but that was before I realized that it was due tomorrow. So I was wondering if he could come to the house for us to work on it."

"A study session huh."

"Yes. If that's a problem I can let him know."

"Oh honey it's not a problem. I don't mind at all. You are eighteen. I told you this was your house and you could do as you pleased."

Aunt Darcy was always so nice to me, and I loved her for it.

"I know. I just didn't want to bother you." I replied.

"No bother at all dear."

"Thank you. I'll be home soon."

"Can't wait to see the hottie," she teased.

"Oh dear."

"No worries. I won't embarrass you. I swear."

"See you soon." I giggled.

"Bye dear."

I hung up the phone and took a deep breath. This would be the first time I'd ever had a boy in my house, also the first time being alone with one. Well, besides my dad and brother. This was big. My heart was racing. I had to keep telling myself that this was no big deal.

I walked back to the table where Jackson was buried deep inside his books. He didn't even hear me walk up.

"Jackson." I called out his name.

"Shit," he called out. "I didn't know you were standing there." Shit must've been his favorite word.

"Sorry." I apologized.

He waved his hand as if not to worry.

"I spoke with my aunt and she said it'd be fine for us to work on your paper."

I saw his shoulders sag in relief. "Awesome. Thank you. You don't know what this means to me."

"You're welcome. I have to get back to work. I have lots of stuff to do before we close."

The next hour flew by. I checked out the last few people and finished off my checklist of things to do. Kennedy finished putting the last of the books back and we walked out together, with Jackson following us.

"Why don't you ride with me to drop Kennedy off at home, and then you can show me where you live." Jackson suggested.

I wanted to politely decline, but I really had no reason. I nodded my head and followed them to the car. Once the door was unlocked, I slid myself into the back seat and fastened my seat belt.

"How are you liking things so far?" Kennedy asked from the seat in front of me.

"I'm adjusting I guess." I looked up from my hands to see Jackson glance back at me.

"You should come hang out with me and my friends sometime."

I wondered if she was talking about the same friends who looked at me like I had two heads the other night at the movies. If that were the case then I'd pass.

"Or the two of us could just hang out." She said, when I hadn't replied.

"Sure. Sounds like fun." I smiled. "Is it just the two of you guys or do you have more brothers and sisters?" I asked turning the conversation to them.

"We have another brother. Tucker is older though, he doesn't live at home." Kennedy answered.

I let out a soft snicker.

"What's so funny?" Jackson asked.

"I just figured if you had another sibling that their name would be Lincoln or something." I laughed. Truthfully, I cracked myself up.

Kennedy leaned her head around the seat and gave me a funny look. Maybe it was because I had a weird laugh, because honestly I did.

"Sorry." I said, covering my mouth.

She busted out laughing, and shook her head. "We've heard that a time or two. Right Jack."

Jackson smiled back at me. "Tucker is sort of the black sheep." He admitted. "His name is fitting."

We pulled into a long driveway that led to a two-story home that could only be described as mansion like. It was huge. I'd seen homes like this before, but never knew the people that lived inside. It was almost dark out, but with the fancy lighting outside I could plainly see the place and just how beautiful it was.

I was still gawking out the window when Kennedy tapped on it from outside. "Nice place." I said as I opened the door.

"Thanks. You can get up front now."

I closed my door and grabbed her door that she was standing next too it.

"I won't be at work for the next couple of days, so I guess I'll see you Sunday." She said.

"Okay. Have a good weekend."

"You too," she winked before walking away.

"You getting in." Jackson called out.

I moved swiftly inside and shut the door. I still could not take my eyes off of their house. I swear my head was glued to the window. The second story had a huge balcony that overlooked the front yard. It had a really pretty white railing on it that looked like it was carved in some intricate design, and I wondered what it would look like up close.

I heard Jackson chuckle from the seat next to me.

"I'll take you in for a tour next time." He said.

I looked over his face and then back to the house. *Next time,* I wondered. "Okay," was my only response as we backed out to leave?

The drive was quiet as we made our way back through town and past the library.

"It's only about two more blocks from here."

"Okay," he replied.

We passed through the last stop sign and I pointed to Aunt Darcy's place. "Just there."

He pulled his car up to the curb and parked directly behind Aunt Darcy.

The quietness between us was a bit unnerving. It didn't calm my already upset stomach. It made it worse. He followed me up the broken pathway and onto the porch. I used my key to open the door, and walked us inside.

"This is nice." He said.

"Thanks." I said. "We can study in the kitchen."

"Sounds good." He followed me there.

"Aunt Darcy," I called out.

"Coming dear." She yelled from the back room.

Jackson stood stoic in the doorway of the kitchen, never saying a word. He seemed much more relaxed then me.

"You can sit your stuff down over on the table. Would you like something to drink?"

"Water would be good."

"Sure." I grabbed two bottles of water from the fridge.

"Hey guys," Darcy said as she walked into the kitchen. She pulled me into a brief hug, which still felt awkward to me. I didn't know if I'd ever get used to it.

"This is Jackson." I introduced him as he walked from around the table and held out his hand.

"Nice to meet you Jackson. I'm Darcy, Grace's aunt." She smiled and took his hand.

"Nice to meet you." He replied.

"I'll let you guys study. I'm going to be doing some laundry, so if it gets too noisy then you all can study in your room." She glanced up at me.

"Ooookay." I said not meaning to sound like an idiot.

She gave me a big, goofy grin. "Nice to meet you Jackson. Hopefully I'll see you again some time." She called out over her shoulder as she walked back down the hall.

"You too." He said back to her.

"Sorry about that." I said.

"She seems nice."

"She really is."

"So where is the rest of your family? I mean your mom and dad." He questioned as we took our seats at the table.

"My mom, dad, and brother all live in Oklahoma."

He eyebrows peeked with curiosity. "So what made you want to move here?"

"It's really complicated. I just needed to get away."

He obviously sensed my unease. "Sorry." He said solemnly.

I shook my head and brushed it off, because he would've had no idea the complications that my past held. He was just striking up conversation.

We spent the next hour and a half talking about Jane Eyre and it had taken me that long to break down the story. We hadn't even touched on really writing the paper yet. It was going to be a long night.

"It sounds like a really sad story." He said, catching me off guard.

I felt myself being sucked in by his words. His curiosity. He had really been listening as I was rambling on and on about the book, and there was such sadness behind his eyes. I barely knew this guy, but one thing I did know was that I'd never seen this kind of emotion from him before, or any emotion for that matter. He seemed like the type that wouldn't let down his guard, so strong and outspoken. He had never been this real with me.

I liked it.

It made him appear not to be so masculine.

His smile stretched wide across his face when he caught me really staring at him. It embarrassed me a little, but I shook it off.

"It is sad." I responded. "But it's also classic love at its best."

I leaned back in my chair and stretched my arms wide over my head. We'd been sitting there for a long time and muscles had grown stiff.

"Do you want to take a break?" He asked.

"Yes," I said too quickly, causing him to laugh.

We stood up from our chairs and walked back to the patio. It was my favorite place. His hand gently brushed the small of my back as we maneuvered around the patio furniture. My body tightened, because I wasn't expecting the small gesture. I hoped he didn't notice my frigidness.

I found myself watching him as his arms stretched high above his head. His shirt slowly rose up and I could see the tanned, tight skin underneath.

"Like what you see?" He asked.

"Uh," I choked and looked anywhere but at him.

"I'm teasing you." His hand caught my elbow and I looked back at him.

"Right." I said. Teasing me.

My face was probably lit up red, but I tried to hide it. There were so many emotions going on in my head, and all of them led back to this one guy. I stared ahead and didn't say anything more. I just wanted to get this night over with and mark it down as a mission accomplished. *Well, sort of.* I laughed out loud at my thoughts, and hoped that he wouldn't read too much into it. He seemed to analyze my every move, and it was intense at times. So much so, that it would leave me flustered and withdrawn. I was acutely unaware of the emotions he brought out in me, and scared to say the least.

free

10

Jackson

"Do you always wear skirts like that?" I asked pointing at the yellow and white skirt that flowed around her ankles.

"Yeah."

"Never pants, or jeans," I eyed her curiously.

"No."

"Why?" My tone sounded a bit more clipped than I expected. I wasn't trying to push. I was just curious.

"It's just the way I was raised. I don't know. No one has ever asked me before." She said.

"Do you want to wear something different?" I asked.

She let out a soft laugh, and I loved it. I loved hearing her laugh. It was so hearty and deep, so much different than you would expect from looking at her.

"No I don't. I like how I look and what I wear. It doesn't bother me, so I never care if it bothers anyone else. People have always looked at me differently. I don't plan on changing myself just to please other people. I am what I am."

"So you don't care what anyone thinks of you."

"Nope." She smiled. "Come on. We better get back to work."

"Yeah okay."

She was so different. I'm not even sure different was the right word for her. She was bold in her own way. She wasn't like any of the girls I'd ever been around before. Never had I ever heard a girl say that they didn't care what other people thought of them. It was just weird, and it didn't go unnoticed that she was so uptight around me either. She flinched every time I touched her, but for some reason I couldn't stop touching her. I found every excuse to do it.

Earlier while I listened to her talk about Jane Eyre I was so engrossed in everything that she said. I never once thought about anything else. But the moment she'd quit talking, I would find myself staring at her lips, or her eyes, or the tiny little lines on her forehead. She really was beautiful.

"Do you mind if we move upstairs now? These chairs really hurt my ass."

Her eyes grew wide.

"I just want comfort. That's all. Hell the couch would be fine with me."

"We can go upstairs." She pushed in her chair and started out of the kitchen. I followed closely behind her.

She reached for and turned on the light inside her bedroom. I was surprised at the sight of it. The walls looked freshly painted and there was nothing hung on them. The dresser was bare, and even the floors.

"Are you sure this is your room?" I asked, looking around.

She nodded and a wide smile spread across her face.

"Grace… The room is empty."

"And," she said.

"And it looks like you moved out, not in." I admitted.

"I don't have much stuff."

"You don't have anything."

I walked over to her full size bed and laid down my things on the light gray comforter. Her bed was freshly made, not a wrinkle in it. She was truly baffling me in every way.

"Look Jackson, I know we don't know each other well, but what you see is what you get with me. I'm just a simple kind of girl. This is the way I dress; this is the way I live." She said as she pointed around the room. "I'm not ashamed. I like it this way." She confessed. "Honestly I don't know any other way. I've had nothing to compare my life too."

I bit down hard on the inside of my jaw as I thought about what she was saying. I guess I wasn't too far off with my "Little House on the Prairie" theory.

"I get it Grace. It's not a big deal. I've just never known anyone quite like you. That's all. If this is what you like then great. I'll try not to be so hard on you. I like to joke and mess around. That's all." I hoped that she wasn't taking me too seriously. She really seemed nice a different and I felt comfortable around her, like I didn't have to try so hard. I could just be myself.

She smiled. "I get that. I've been around you long enough now to realize that." Her laughter filled the room. "I just wanted you to know. You can make assumptions or joke all you want. I can take it. I'm a big girl."

"Yes you are." And she was all right. "Now lets get this paper done."

"Yes. Let's…"

I watched her as she slipped off her little white shoes and socks and climbed up on the bed. She had the tiniest little feet. She had to be tiny under that skirt. I bet she had a kicking little body too, all tight and shit. I had to shift around to keep from growing an erection in front of her innocent eyes.

It took us two more hours to finish the paper but we did it, and damn it, I was impressed. This was a good paper, and I had her to thank for it. She helped me in every way. She was a great teacher. There was no way that I was ever going to read Jane Eyre, but truthfully she made it very interesting for me. Something I never thought would happen. Hell, I wouldn't even take literature under normal circumstances. My counselor suggested it. She said it'd be easy. I did like to read, but only things with adventure and action.

My phone rang from inside my backpack and I fished it out to see who it was. When I saw Holly's name on the screen I quickly hit reject and tossed it back in. I had spent the last three hours in a whiny free zone. I couldn't handle her. The bitching and complaining would be too much for me to take. For the moment, I was enjoying the peacefulness of Grace's company.

"I bet you get an A on that paper." She said breaking me from my thoughts.

"He'd be stupid not to give me an A."

"Absolutely." She nodded her head in agreement. Her smile was bright and eyes so engaging. They were a dark blue, almost midnight color. But at times, when she would turn her head just right I could see a tiny hint of green. They were penetrating and gorgeous. There was so much light inside of her. It shined bright through her eyes. She was exactly what happiness would look like, if it had a face.

I watched her as she yawned and leaned her body back against the headboard.

"I should get going."

"Okay." She said. "I'll walk you out."

I grabbed my bag off the floor and followed her down the stairs to the front door.

"I had a nice time Jackson." She admitted a little sheepishly.

"You know what?" I slid past her and stepped on to the porch. "I did too. I really did." I smiled. I didn't tell her what I was really thinking. If she saw right through my devilish grin, she never said. I couldn't help myself. Despite her lack of know how, she was mesmerizing. I wanted to be next to her. I wanted to touch her. It was probably best that I was leaving, otherwise I would find some way to persuade her to do dirty things that her innocent mind knew nothing about.

"Really." She cocked her head to the side. "Who knew that I could be so much fun?" Her voice was high pitched. She was clearly mocking me.

"Wow, I didn't know that you were funny too." I joked back.

She shook her head. "Goodnight Jackson. Let me know how you do on the paper."

"I will." I quickly kissed her cheek before she realized what I was doing, and before she had the chance to slam the door shut in my face. "Thank you." I said waving goodbye and walking away.

I wanted so badly to kick up my heels as I walked to my car, because the look on her face was priceless. She didn't expect me to do that. Hell, I didn't even expect it. It was just my way of saying thank you.

Okay, not really. Truthfully I'd wanted to do that all night, but knew she'd probably freak out. Not only were my hands drawn to her, so were my lips. When I turned around to steal one last glance at her my smile widened.

She stood there in the door jam with her hand against the cheek where I kissed her. She was staring straight at me. I had shocked the hell out of her. Her face was blank. Shit. Maybe I'd frightened her. That wasn't what I was trying to do.

I chanced a wave, and let out my breath when she waved back with a tiny smile on her face.

Victory was mine.

Taking a seat behind the wheel, I drove off with the biggest smile on my face.

11

Grace

Holy crap.

I locked the door behind me as I ran to my room as quickly as I could. My cheek was still warm or maybe it was my blood pressure. I didn't know. All I knew was that he kissed me.

He freaking kissed me.

Did I like it?

Was I angry?

Would I let him do it again?

Yes, no, and definitely yes.

I wanted to scream. It was my first kiss. Well, not really kiss because his lips never touched mine. But I didn't care. I was counting it.

There was no way I could sleep after that.

First I wanted to write about it, and then I wanted to tell to Darcy.

I bounced around the room and grabbed my poetry book from my dresser. My heart was still racing and I'd never felt this excited about anything.

Opening the book, I turned to the first blank page and started writing.

Jackson

My face was heated. My soul was touched.

His kiss was tender, soft, and warm.

Sometimes the most unexpected things brought us happiness.

I'd never met anyone like him. I'd never known they existed.

He was cocky, blunt, and full of life.

He made me look at things differently in an unusual light.

I didn't know him. I barely knew myself.

I only knew that I liked his company, enjoyed his laugh, and loved that kiss.

Jackson made me feel different, but in a good way.

What would I take away from this? What would I gain?

Absolutely nothing.

Absolutely everything.

Today was my first kiss.

His name was Jackson.

I'd thank him one day.

Thank him for my first act of freedom.

Thank him for not being scared.

Thank him for stealing that kiss.

Thank him for trusting me.

Thank him for asking questions.

Thank him for listening as I spoke.

Thank him for being himself.

If I never saw him again, that would be okay.

I'd never forget today.

Jackson.

I sighed as I closed the book.

"Oh world." I said. "Just try taking this smile off my face. I dare you."

I sprang down the stairs and ran straight into Darcy's room. She patted the bed and I jumped onto it excitedly. I spent the next hour replaying the entire night. She listened to my every word and only commented a few times with the occasional "Oh, or he had the cutest smile, or I'm so happy for you."

I realized that these were probably the talks that thirteen-year-old girls had with their best friends. It couldn't possibly be the conversation between an eighteen-year-old and her aunt.

Still. I didn't care. My life was only just beginning. Other girls were probably miles ahead of me in their lives, but I wasn't other girl's. And I didn't care what anyone thought of me. This was freedom at its best.

I am Free!"

It was Saturday. I didn't have to work and Aunt Darcy was spending the day with Paul and told me to do whatever I wanted. I was content with spending hours in front of the television.

Literally, it was hours.

I watched three movies and some crazy show where they took some old run down house and remodeled it to sale. It was amazing. Seriously. It only took them like a week to rebuild an entire house.

About halfway through my bag of potato chips and the second episode of the house makeover show, I heard someone knock on the door. My heart dropped to my butt. Instantly I thought maybe it would be my father, and I started to have a mini panic attack. I tiptoed around the couch as if the person standing outside the door might hear me. Not likely, but I couldn't help freaking out.

"Get a grip Grace." I said to myself. It couldn't be my father. He had no idea where I was. Surely he wouldn't come looking for me. Just as I stepped closer to the door, whoever was behind it knocked again. Then a voice yelled out.

"Grace, come on open up. It's me Kennedy." She called out.

I let out the biggest sigh ever as I swung open the door.

"Hey," I smiled. "What are you doing here?" I asked. I looked at her questionably. "And how'd you know where I lived?"

She pointed her thumb over her shoulder, and when I peeked around I saw Jackson sitting in the driver's seat of his car. He shot me a wave.

I smiled and waved back.

When I looked back at Kennedy, I still had a blank look on my face. Her sheepish grin made me think she was up to something. She was the mischievous sort.

"Well?" I asked.

"I'm sorry to surprise you, but I didn't have your number. I was hoping that we could hang out for a little while. My car will be ready to pick up in a few hours and Jackson is supposed to take me to get it. I was really bored sitting at home."

"Don't you have other friends?" The words slipped from my mouth before I had a chance to realize what I was saying. Stupid. Stupid. Stupid.

Her eyes grew wide, and her mouth dropped open.

"That. Is. Not. What. I. Meant." I paused between each word. "I mean. Ugh," I sighed. I just couldn't understand why she'd want to hang out with me. I knew she had other friends. She'd be just as bored with me as she would be if she were home.

She laughed and patted my shoulder. "I knew what you meant. Do you want to hang out?"

"Sure," I replied with a smile, and opened the door wider. I didn't ask what hanging out would require, and hoped that she secretly loved home makeover shows.

She waved at Jackson and I watched as he pulled away from the curb.

Closing the door behind us, I walked us into the living room.

"My aunt isn't home. It's just me and the T.V." I said.

She made herself comfortable on the couch, pulling her legs up close to her. I sat down next to her and couldn't help admiring the bright red polish on her toes. I loved it.

"Have you ever?" She looked at me and then stretched her legs out to my lap letting out a groan. "Have you ever painted your toes?" She asked obviously catching me staring at them.

"No." I shook my head.

"Want to?" She asked excitedly, a little too excitedly actually. She was extra bubbly at times. I was a fairly happy person myself, but her enthusiasm made things brighter, more cheerful.

"I don't have any."

"That's okay I brought mine." She reached down beside the couch and pulled her purse onto her lap, dumping the contents out everywhere.

"Wow." I laughed. "Is there anything you don't have in there?"

"You can never be too prepared." She batted her dark coated lashes at me.

She dug around until she found what she was looking for.

"Here it is." She held up the bottle of red polish. She moved to sit in front of me on the table and patted her legs for me to give her my feet.

The only color polish I had ever used was clear. My mother never bought colored polish, and I never asked.

With a little too much enthusiasm, I swung my legs up to her lap.

A giggle escaped her lips, and I couldn't contain mine.

"Why do I get the feeling that you've never experienced An Affair in Red Square?" Her voice was thick with a British accent.

"What?" I looked at her funny.

"It's the name of the polish Grace." She dropped her head back down an opened the bottle, still laughing. "Seriously though, this will feel like an act of rebellion, right?"

"A little." I replied sheepishly. It'd be fun though.

"Can I ask you something?"

I could only imagine what would come out of her mouth next. Was I prepared for it? Did I want to talk about my home life and my past? I nodded my head. I wouldn't give her all of the crappy details, but I've only ever been honest. So I'd tell her whatever she wanted to know.

"What was your home life like in Oklahoma? On our first day at work you told me that you just wanted to experience a little bit of freedom. Was life at home bad?" She asked as she brushed the red polish along my big toe.

She must have sensed my nervousness. My whole body was tense. I was replaying my responses over and over in my head. I didn't want to tell her everything, just enough to suffice her.

She stopped what she was doing and looked up at me. "I'm sorry Grace. If you don't want to talk about it, I understand."

"No, no, it's fine." I leaned back a little on the couch. "My life wasn't bad all the time. It was different; unlike yours I'm sure. I didn't realize how different until I came here. I guess you could say it was very controlled. My dad was strict."

"How strict?" She asked.

"Well," I said afraid to say the rest. If she thought I was innocent, she really had no idea how much. I took a deep breath before replying. "No pants, no bathing suits, no makeup, no cell phone, no internet except for the main computer that my mom schooled me on, but I wasn't allowed to use it, no public school, no boyfriends until after I turned eighteen, no friends outside of our close nit circle which included one girl, and the list goes on and on. We lived on a farm so my days consisted of chores at six a.m. and bed by 8 p.m."

"Wait a minute." She drawled out her words. "Back up. No boyfriends." She exclaimed.

"Nope." I popped the P.

"So you have never had a boyfriend?" Her eyes grew wide as she waited for my answer.

I laughed. "No, no boyfriend. And before you ask, that also means all of the things that go along with it. I haven't dated, held hands, kissed…" I trailed off because I couldn't possibly mention the fact that I had just experienced my first kiss with her brother. I smiled at the thought of it.

"That is sad Grace. You are seriously deprived." Her face fell.

"No I'm not." A small smile crept up on my lips. "So I'm getting a little bit of a late start." I shrugged. "I don't mind. There were very few boys within a twenty-mile radius of my house. I never even cared to date. Besides, I learned a long time ago, that if you never had things then you never missed them. You know?" I explained.

She continued polishing my toes and I didn't say anything for a while. It was the first time that I ever wondered what someone was thinking about me.

"Done." She smiled closing up the bottle of nail polish.

I eyed my toes and wiggled them around. "I love it." I beamed. It was another piece of freedom that I could cross off my list. "Thank you."

Kennedy eyes lit up. "You're welcome. And thanks for sharing all that personal stuff with me. I'm glad you trust me with it."

"We're friends." I urged.

"Yes we are." She agreed. "I would never make fun of who you are Grace. I want you to know that. It's okay that you aren't as experienced as most girls, because then you wouldn't be Grace."

At that moment, I realized that she was the closest friend I'd ever had. I could trust her with anything. I wanted her to hang around, because at this rate we'd be best friends soon. I wanted a best friend, more than anything.

I looked over my toes again. I was in love with the deep red polish that covered them, and she was right when she said it would be rebellious. It felt down right illegal.

"You want something to eat?" I asked.

"Sure, so long as it is full of sugar."

We walked into the kitchen and raided the cabinets for the sweets. Then we went back into the living room and binged out. I loved every minute of it.

The hours passed by so quickly and she said that Jackson was on his way to pick her up. Just the sound of his name peeked my interest.

"Oh my God," she sat up quickly. "I have the best idea ever."

I bit down on my lip and peered up at her. I had a feeling this was going to be bad. Of course it was going to be bad. This was Kennedy after all.

"Come with me and my friends tonight." It was more of a statement than a question.

I was already shaking my head as if it were a bad idea. "I don't think so." I started to oppose.

"Grace," she wined. "You'll have so much fun and you'll be with me all night."

"Where are you going?" I sighed. Her winey voice super annoying, and I would almost do anything to get her to zip it up.

"We are going to a local club that we always hang out at called The Edge." She said and before I could say HECK NO, she interjected. "Hear me out." Her hands rested on my shoulders.

I fought to keep from rolling my eyes at her. Which was normally something she would do. She was rubbing off on me.

"Everybody from school goes to this club. You only have to be eighteen. Nothing bad ever happens. Plus you

will get to hang out with me. It'll be fun. I swear. Please."
She pouted her lip.

The thought of a club scared me a little. I mean I didn't really know what to expect. Whether it would be dangerous or not? Staring at her big lip that stuck out far from her face was killing me. How her parents ever told her no was beyond me.

You're not at home Grace. This is your time to experience life. Quit being such a scaredy pants. The internal battle in my head was going strong.

"Fine. I'll go. But if it's too crazy for me, then I'm going home."

"Eeeep." She squealed wrapping her arms around me in a hug. One of those things that still felt weird and uncomfortable to me. There was a knock on the door and I knew this time that it would be Jackson. "I'll be here at 8:30 to pick you up."

"Oh Kennedy," I called after her.

"Yeah."

"I'm dressing like I always do." I said honestly.

"I know." The smile stretched widely across her face. "See you later."

"See ya." I waved.

I threw myself roughly down on the couch and crossed my arm over my face.

"What am I getting myself into?"

12

Jackson

The club wasn't too crowded yet, as we walked in and found our table. Holly was attached at my hip and had been since I picked her up. I didn't mind too much, because I loved the way her body felt pressed up against mine.

I'd been a little distracted all day after seeing Grace wave to me from her porch. How could such an innocent girl have such an effect on me? It was the question that I'd asked myself time and time again. Yet, I had no answer for it.

The music started from the back of the bar and I pulled Holly in front of me to stand between my legs. Jeremy had already left us as he walked over to the bar to get our drinks. I wanted something warm that would burn as I drank it down.

Jeremy brought back my drink, and we sat there cutting up as the music played. More and more people started piling in through the door. It didn't take long before the place was packed. The weekend crowd was always the biggest. It was really the only place that anyone hung out, at least any of my friends. Nearly all of the guys from the team that I hung out with were hanging out by our table. Girls were everywhere seeking their attention. A part of me wished that I were single again, so that I didn't have to worry about appeasing one girl. I could do what I wanted. I'd at least put more effort into going after the girl that I couldn't stop thinking about. Or would I? Another part of me was glad that Holly was constant in my life. I didn't have to worry about my game, or which hoe I'd take home at the end of that night. It was always her.

A shift in gazes from around the table, made me snap my head around to see what everyone was staring at.

Fuck me.

She was here. Grace was here. Kennedy and her were walking through the crowd of people and over to our table.

I shifted uncomfortably in my seat.

Jokes were being tossed around about her, and I flinched with their hurtful words. But I didn't say anything. I listened as they continued.

"What is she wearing?" I heard.

"She must be looking for her sheep." Someone else said.

"She can't be serious." I heard Holly say, joining in.

Still, I said nothing.

Kennedy and Grace walked up to the table. I glanced nervously down at Holly's back, and then back around the table. I could tell now that the guys were finally seeing Grace's face. They were seeing how beautiful she really was, but that wouldn't stop the jokes.

"Hey guys." Kennedy said.

People were still snickering and staring with their eyes wide.

"Hey Kennedy," Holly said with a thick mean girl accent. "You helping Little Bo Peep find her sheep?" She laughed, and so did the rest of the table.

I should have pushed her off my lap. I should have told her to shut the hell up. I probably should have even defended Grace, but I didn't. I just sat there. I made a quick glance in Grace's direction and could see her eyes focused on my arm, the same arm that was around Holly's waist. I jerked my head around quickly.

"Hey Jackson." Grace said to me in a quiet voice. It was just loud enough that only Holly and me could hear it. I couldn't look up. I didn't have the fucking balls to look up. Everyone was laughing at her. I gave her a quick head nod but didn't bring my eyes anywhere near her face.

I felt Holly lean into me closer when Grace said my name. She was obviously staking claim to me as if she had to worry about Grace. I knew that there was an attraction between Grace and me, but I wasn't about to commit social suicide, at least not in front of anyone.

"Don't be jealous Holly. It doesn't suit you." Kennedy replied.

"Why the hell would I be jealous? I mean look at her." Holly spouted as she pointed in Grace's direction. Her voice rang loudly over the room, and caused unnecessary attention.

"Maybe because she doesn't have to get her blonde hair from a bottle, or maybe it's because she's not even wearing makeup and she's prettier than you'll ever be."

I felt Holly's body tense against mine. She squeezed my thigh hard like she wanted me to step in and say something.

Oh hell no.

She got herself into that mess, and I wasn't about to start a fight with my sister.

"Grace," Kennedy said loudly. "These are the ass holes," she waved her arms around the table. "And Ass holes," she was talking to us as a crowd. "This is Grace. Come on Grace. Let's go. I will introduce you to some people with class." Kennedy grabbed Grace's arm and pulled her away.

There was still a smile on her face. Even after the way Holly had spoken to her, and the way everyone else laughed at her. She was still smiling. I felt bad. I felt like the ass hole that Kennedy said I was.

But I didn't feel bad enough to chase after her and apologize.

Holly turned around to me and gave me the meanest look. I just shrugged my shoulders, and didn't say another word. I tipped up my glass, and finished off the entire thing.

I left Holly at the table sulking while I walked off to the bathroom. I'd already finished two glasses of whiskey and some nasty shot of something. I was unsteady on my feet. When I made it to the edge of the dance floor I found myself drawn to the blonde by the bar. Looking harder I realized it was Grace. She and Kennedy were standing there at the corner talking to a couple of guys. It was harmless, but I could feel a twinge of jealousy inside me. I didn't want anyone else talking to Grace. Not only that, they were laughing. Not at her like I had done. They were laughing with her as if she'd told a funny joke. Was she funny?

I let out a loud groan and ran my fingers through my hair as I stomped off to the bathroom. There were too many emotions running through me, and I didn't know what to make of them all. I had no right to be jealous. I couldn't even explain to myself why I'd even felt that way to begin with.

I splashed some cool water on my face from the sink in the bathroom. All I wanted to do was go home. Or go home with Holly. Actually, that plan sounded a lot better.

Stepping out of the bathroom, I started walking back to the table. Well, that was what my intentions were, but I found myself walking straight towards Kennedy and Grace. The two guys eyed me curiously when I stepped up in between the two girls. My face was hard and my eyes glared at them. I was so angry with them that I couldn't see straight. I wanted to stack claim here and tell them to walk out those doors and never look back, but I didn't.

"Problem?" One of the guys said to me. I bit down hard on my lip to keep myself together. I didn't like these assholes. Not one, single, bit.

"There'd better not be, seeing as you're talking to my girls." I spat out.

Kennedy sighed. "Seriously Jackson. Go away." She whispered in my ear.

"You know this guy?" The prick asked Kennedy.

"You could say that." She paused. "He's my brother."

I could see the look on the guys face turn from frigid dickhead to sincere schoolboy.

Yep. That's right buddy. I'm the big bad brother. What are you going to do now?

"He was just leaving." Kennedy groaned. She turned to face me and put her finger on my chest. "Go home Jackson. You're drunk. I'm old enough to take care of myself. Don't think I don't know exactly why you're acting like an idiot. I'm not stupid, and I'm not going to say it out loud." Her eyes narrowed and I could see an understanding in them. She understood me better than I did at that moment. "Now walk your drunk ass back to your table with you girlfriend, and leave us alone. Better yet Jack, go home." She gave me a hard shove backwards and I stumbled barely able to stand.

I looked over at Grace and saw pain on her face. Was it my fault? She looked kind of sad and she was fidgeting. I probably looked so stupid in front of her.

"Fine," I yelled out and walked away. I walked away and left them there with those guys even though every part of me didn't want to.

Grabbing Holly by the wrist, I pulled her close to me.

"Take me to your place." I said in a low whisper.

"Lead the way."

free

13

Grace

I had no idea what just happened, but it scared me a bit. We were just talking to these guys and Jackson made such a scene. He'd obviously had way too much to drink. Kennedy knew just how to handle him because with a few words she was able to get him to leave. Not just us, but he left the entire bar. I watched him as he left with Holly under his arm. I didn't ask Kennedy about her, but I wanted to. It was obvious that Holly and Jackson was a couple.

Kennedy took up for me when Holly and the rest of the table were laughing at me, but I later told her that it wasn't necessary. She didn't have to come to my defense, because I never cared what anyone thought of me. Maybe it was years of obedience that my parents hammered into my brain. Looks were never an issue, and neither were materialistic things. We'd always been looked at differently back home. Even in the grocery store, people would laugh and point. My mom always told me to hold my head high. That being different was okay. As long as we didn't have a problem with it, then no one else should either. I guess what she said always stuck with me. Sometimes situations would become uncomfortable just like earlier tonight when we stood at the table with all the "ass-holes" as Kennedy called them. I kept a smile on my face so that they would know that their words were petty, that they didn't bother me at all. The only thing that did bother me was the way that Jackson acted. It was as if he didn't know who I was. I shrugged it off. I thought maybe because Kennedy was so excepting of me, that maybe he would be too. I was completely wrong. I suppose he only wanted to be friends with me when no one was looking, or when he needed something.

I wanted to laugh at the thought. I wanted to just say grow up, and was glad when Kennedy had pulled me away from them.

The guys that we'd been talking to seemed not to care. They were very nice. Kennedy made it so easy for me. She introduced me and did most of the talking. I was never uneasy or pressured, and they were both very nice. Too be honest, I thought maybe they were a whole lot older than Jackson and his friends because they didn't act so childish. It was a nice change of pace.

Well, up until Jackson came to ruin it.

"I'm so sorry about that. He's very drunk and he gets a little overprotective."

"It's okay." Adam said. He was the tall guy that clearly had his eyes on Kennedy.

His friend Preston was really nice too. He never made jokes or laughed at me. We had real, adult conversation. We talked about his job and how he worked all the time. We also talked about my love for poetry which I never really talked much about before. He loved art and so one subject led to the next. Before I knew it we were laughing and having a great time.

"We have to be going because I have to be at work early in the morning." Preston said. He took my hand and shook it telling me how nice it was to meet me, and it was. It was very nice.

I noticed that Kennedy and Adam were exchanging numbers and I thought maybe that was what I should be doing with Preston, but I'm kind of glad he didn't suggest it. Baby steps were best for me, and I was in no way ready to start going on real dates.

We said our goodbyes and Kennedy asked if I was ready to leave too. I nodded and followed her as she led us out the doors into the cool night air.

"So," she beamed locking her arm through mine as we walked through the parking lot. "What did you think?"

I leaned my head over to rest on her shoulder. I couldn't keep the smile off my face. "I had a great time."

"YES!" She yelled out. "I knew that you would. I told you I would introduce you to some people with class didn't I?" She hummed proudly as we made our way to the car.

"Yes you did, and the guys were nice. I hope that you'll let me go with you again sometime?" I suggested. I knew that her other friends were supposed to go with us tonight, and I had a horrible feeling that they backed out because of me. Why? I didn't know. Maybe they didn't want to be seen with me, or maybe they were worried that I was moving in on their best friend. I really had no idea, because I had nothing to compare this too. Everything was new to me.

"Are you kidding me? Of course we'll go again. I love having you around. I don't have to try so hard with you."

"What do you mean?" I asked as we reached the car.

"You saw the way those ass-holes acted in there." She said and I nodded. "My friends are no different Grace. I can't stand it. Maybe I'm an outsider just like you, because I don't give two shits about their fancy cars or their snobby attitudes or even their daddy's money. I'm not going to be in this damn city forever and all I want is to be real. This fake shit gets on my nerves." She winked at me and we climbed into the car.

She was so refreshing. I think I was beginning to love her. Not like love her love her, but like a best friend kind of love.

"I'm sorry about the way my brother and his girlfriend acted."

And there was the magic G word.

I shrugged my shoulders. "Don't worry about it. You think I haven't heard it before? I've been called everything." I waved her off.

"That doesn't hurt you at all?" She turned around to face me in her seat. "Honestly Grace. How can that not bother you?"

"There was probably a time when it did many years ago, but not now. I love me, all of me. I love my shoes that have laces and my plain white socks. I love my skirts and my sweaters. I love that I have never once said the F word. I love that I haven't had sex yet. I love that I now have my very first best friend and I am eighteen years old." I smiled. "I'd love to tell you about my home life some time when I'm ready, but for now just know that I'm fine. I'm free."

Her head leaned over against the headrest beside her. She smiled. I knew that she was probably wondering what I meant. She was probably running every crazy scenario through her head about my home life, but she never asked. "I love being your very first best friend." She admitted.

"Me too. Now take me somewhere for some greasy food would ya?" I laughed and buckled my seat belt.

"You got it." She started the car. "Hey."

"What?" I asked.

"I hope now that you've seen his true colors that you'll be over my brother." She stated matter of fact. I felt the lump in my stomach all the way down to my butt. How the heck did she know that?

Please let this be the last time she brings this up. I thought to myself.

"Hard to be over him, when I was never under him." I replied.

Her eyes widened. "Why little Grace, did you just make your first obscene joke?"

"What can I say? You're rubbing off on me." I laughed as we pulled out of the parking lot. We giggled all the way to nearest drive-thru.

i am *free*

14

Jackson

It was Wednesday, and I was sitting in the parking lot at school with my Lit paper in my hands, the paper that Grace had helped me write. Written in red sharpie on the top was my Grade. I'd gotten an A-. This was the best grade I had gotten on a paper since I'd been in college, and I owed it all to Grace. I had to share it with her.

I drove the few minutes to the library hoping that she'd be working.

I took the steps to the building two at a time. Opening the glass door, I searched for her. She wasn't behind the front desk. I didn't see anyone there. I walked through every roll of books until I finally spotted her. She had her back to me and was searching through a cart of books. I ran to her quickly not thinking about what I was doing. I grabbed her around the waist and lifted her off of the ground spinning her around.

She let out a loud squeal, and slapped my hand.

"Grace it's me." I said putting her back on her feet.

"Jackson." She heaved a sigh of relief. "You scared me."

"I'm sorry."

Her already pale face was even more ghostly. Her hand was still over her obviously racing heart when she finally looked at the paper I was holding out in front of me.

Her lip rose up a little on the corners, but it was half hearted. I thought she'd be happier than this. I thought that she'd be as happy as I was, overjoyed even.

"That's great Jackson." She said just above a whisper and turned back around to the bookshelf.

"What's wrong Grace? Aren't you happy for me?" I asked. This wasn't the usual Grace that I was used to seeing. Normally she'd be smiling and full of life. Something was wrong with her.

"Yeah Jackson. Good job." She said half-heartedly.

"You don't sound too happy."

She turned on her heels and looked me straight in the eyes. "I guess I wasn't aware that we were speaking again." Her eyes narrowed and she frowned.

Damn it, that hurt. "I deserve that."

"Look it's okay. I don't care that you're ashamed to be friends with me, but I'm not stooping to your level. This is my first chance at normalcy and I'd much rather spend it with people who are real."

"Grace." I spoke her name and could see the effect that it had on her. She loved hearing me say her name as much as much as I loved saying it. "I'm sorry."

"I said it was okay. I don't need or expect an apology from you, especially if you don't mean it. I'm glad that you passed your essay, and I'll help you anytime you need it. But let's don't pretend to be friends when we're not."

I swallowed the massive lump in my throat. It felt like I'd been punched in the gut, but I deserved it. I don't know why I acted like such a douche to her. She'd never done anything to deserve it. She'd been nothing but amazing to me, and I repaid her by pretending that I didn't even know her. When all I really wanted to do was actually know her.

I placed my hand on her shoulder and felt her body tense underneath my hand.

"I have to get back to work." She quickly pushed the cart away and said nothing else. What else could she say? She didn't owe me anything and she'd spoken her peace.

I walked out of the building the same way I'd came in, and I didn't look back.

First I was angry with myself for treating her like that, then I was angry with Kennedy for introducing me to her, and then I was angry with Grace for being such a do-gooder. Too much time had passed with my mind focused solely on her, and I wasn't wasting one more second. I knew that I'd never have a chance with her, and subconsciously I think I only wanted to sleep with her. At least that was what I was telling myself. It was fun while it lasted.

"Later Grace." I flipped up the deuces as I walked down the steps of the library. I didn't want to think about Little Bo Peep again.

15

Grace

The weeks had passed by so quickly. I loved my job and had picked up all the hours that Trish would allow. I was there more often than not, which was perfectly fine by me. I loved the money and the comfort of having a routine. Kennedy and I were still having the best time. She hung out with me a lot at the house, and Aunt Darcy loved her. We went on shopping trips, movie trips, and even trips to the salon. She had paid for me to have my first pedicure, and I got my hair trimmed by someone other than my mom. It was perfect, sort of. I doubt that I'll be having any more pedicures anytime soon. I didn't realize I was so ticklish and it was hard communicating with the lady because she didn't speak English. I could mark it off of my freedom list, but wouldn't be experiencing it again any time soon.

I'd just gotten off the phone with Kennedy who was on her way over with exciting news. I wasn't sure what that meant, and by the tone of her voice I was a little scared. She was the most unpredictable person I'd ever met, and the funniest.

There was a knock on the door, but I didn't bother getting off the couch. Kennedy would just walk on in liked she owned the place.

"Guess what?" She hopped onto the couch next to me. I was too busy staring at her breasts to guess.

Holy crap, where was the rest of her shirt?

"You like." She wiggled her chest in front of me.

I laughed. "I hope you didn't pay full price for that. They forgot some material." I joked. I loved being able to be myself around her. I didn't even realize how funny I actually was until Kennedy came into my life.

"Ha ha," She rolled her eyes. "But really, guess what?"

"I'll never guess it right, so just tell me and save us both the trouble."

"We have a date." She squealed.

I'm pretty sure that was the exact moment that I'd forgotten how to breathe. I couldn't get it right. Was it in and out, or out than in.

She grabbed me by my shoulders and gave me a little shake. "Pull yourself together woman."

"A date." I could feel the look of horror all over my face.

She nodded. "With Adam and Preston. A double date," she explained.

I let out my breath. Whew. I guess I knew how to breathe after all.

"Let's go to my house and get ready." She jumped up grabbing my arm.

"Wait. Are you sure that I'm wanted on this date? I mean this isn't some pity thing were Preston and I are needed for some kind of friend diversion?"

"What?" She laughed. "What the hell is a friend diversion?"

"You know like you can't go on your date without having a friend with you as backup." I explained. How did I know that, and she didn't?

"I have got to get you away from the television. It's seriously frying that gorgeous brain of yours. Now stop fretting. When Adam called me earlier he said that Preston wanted to ask you himself, but since he had no way of contacting you, he left Adam to do his dirty work. They both want us to come out. So we are going."

I grinned sheepishly. "My first real date."

"Yes, now go get your stuff and lets go."

I made it to my room and back in record time. I was more excited about the date then I realized, and this was the first time that I was going to be inside of Kennedy's house. For some reason that excited me too.

We made the drive to her house and when we pulled into the driveway I suddenly got nervous. I hadn't seen Jackson in weeks, and I was worried that I'd run into him. If I did, what would I say? How would he act? I hesitated before getting out of the car.

"He's not here." She eyed me curiously.

"Are you telepathic or something?"

Kennedy put her arm around me. "No, but your expressions are easy to read. It's one of the many things I love about you. Now come on."

She put her key in the lock and turned the knob to the front door. The noise was crazy loud. I arched an eyebrow at her wondering what was going on. It sounded like there was a concert coming from somewhere inside the house. She rolled her eyes and led me into the largest sitting room I'd ever seen. Seriously, my bedroom would have fit inside of it five times. My mouth dropped open when I saw a guy standing on the floor in front of the television holding a plastic colorful guitar and banging his head to what I then realized was the concert coming from the T.V.

I couldn't contain the laughter that escaped my mouth. He was like a rock star or something.

Kennedy walked over to the remote and hit a button causing the room to grow silent. The tall guy with the shaggy hair started to say something to her, which I figured wouldn't be nice, but that was until he spotted me. A large playful grin spread across his beautiful face, and he had the cutest dimples I'd ever seen.

"Grace, come meet my other brother Tucker." She waved me over.

"Hey Gracie," he said with a sugary tone and I was flattered all the way to my toes. Good looks obviously ran in this family. He was clearly much older that Kennedy and Jackson, but still super cute.

He held out a hand to me and I placed mine inside it. "Hey, nice to meet you Tucker," I said.

"Aren't you the cutest thing ever?" He gloated still holding my hand in his.

I wanted to say likewise, but didn't have the guts. His harmless flirting was already making me a weakling.

"She is also too young for you." Kennedy growled at him, taking my hand out of his.

Tucker was still smiling at me as Kennedy pulled me away quickly. "Nice to meet you Tucker." I called after him.

"You too beautiful."

"Do not pay any attention to him. Please." Kennedy explained.

"He's harmless," I said. "And very cute."

"And too old for you." She said.

"I know. I'm just stating the obvious."

She shook her head. "I really am rubbing off on you."

Up the stairs, to the right, and at the end of the long hallway was Kennedy's bedroom. Or should I say Kennedy's apartment. This place had everything. There was an attached bathroom with a shower and a tub the size of a small swimming pool. She had a small balcony, and there was a mini fridge next to her closet. I couldn't stop myself from opening it. I had to see what was inside.

There were Mt. Dews, bottled water, and Reese cups.

"The necessities," she said tossed her stuff on the floor like it was no big deal.

"Since when is caffeine and chocolate a necessity?" I asked.

"Since forever." She gave me a weird look. "You were deprived as a kid, and don't tell me you weren't. That's my theory and I'm sticking to it."

I just laughed. I knew I wasn't deprived. We had sweets and caffeine sometimes, especially during holidays. My childhood wasn't awful –at least not always, just very strict and defined. If my father had never hit me, I'd probably still be there, despite my indifferences and their beliefs.

"Let's change and get ready."

She started stripping off her clothes right there in front of me.

I gave her an awkward glance.

"Oh come on Grace. We are both girls. I have seen all the girlie parts there are to see, yours will be no different."

That's easy for her to say. She stood there, bare chest, and she was beautiful. I was as modest as they came.

I turned my back to her and lifted the shirt over my head. If she could do it, then so could I. Kind of. I kept my back facing her so that she wouldn't get a frontal view. I wasn't quite ready to jump all in.

"Grace. Oh my God."

Realization hit me.

The scars.

She saw my scars.

Crap. I'd been so worried about her seeing my front that I hadn't even thought about my back. No one had seen those scars, but my mother. It was the worst memory I'd had of my father, and I was in no way ready to relive that day yet. Not with myself, and definitely not with Kennedy. Not yet.

"What happened to you?" She asked. There was concern in her voice.

Of course there was concern. She was my friend. I took a deep breath trying to think of the right thing to say to keep her from asking too much.

"Remember that home life I didn't want to talk about?" I said. I turned to face her and saw the sadness in her eyes. She nodded her head in understanding. She didn't speak.

"I still don't want to talk about it." I admitted.

There was a long awkward pause from her as she looked over my bare body. There was a brief moment where I actually thought she might cry. I was shocked when all she said was, "Okay." That was it. There was no added pressure on me. She didn't ask any other questions, but I could tell that she wanted to. It wasn't something that I was ready to discuss yet. I wasn't sure if I'd ever be ready.

With a hint of a smile on my face, I tried to reassure her. I wanted her to know that if I ever did want to talk about that she'd be the one that I'd tell. I trusted her that much. Reaching for her hand and squeezing it in mine I whispered. "Come on. Let's finish getting ready. I'll let you see my boobs." I couldn't contain the laughter that escaped my lips.

She laughed too. The tension in the room was finally lifted. The conversation wasn't over. I knew that. But for a moment it wasn't going to be thought about. That was all I could ask for.

Kennedy wore this beautiful green dress that of course showed way too much skin but she looked gorgeous. Her hair was curled and pinned back from her face. I wore a dark gray top that my Aunt Darcy had bought me that was a little bit form fitting to my body, and it had a high neckline. It was beautiful and I couldn't wait to have some place nice to wear it to. I could in no way compare myself to Kennedy, but I felt pretty, and that was all that mattered.

We talked about the night as I sat on Kennedy's bathroom sink and watched her spend thirty minutes putting on her makeup. It was unbelievable the amount of work it took. It seemed easy to do, but there were so many items that she put on. I couldn't keep up. And I had no clue how she kept from poking her eyes out.

The last thing that she put on was lipstick. It was bright red, and amazing. I loved it. She caught me eyeing it, and slid the tube in my direction.

"Try it on, Gracie." She over exaggerated the name that Tucker had given me earlier. "It's not dangerous, it's beautiful." She smiled.

I pinched my lips together tightly thinking about it, before jumping off the bathroom counter. In two shaky movements, I had the prettiest lips I'd ever seen.

"Perfect." Kennedy said. "You ready to go?"

Was I? Would I actually go out of the house with this stuff on?

Yes I would. "Let's go. I'm ready." I popped my lips and smiled big.

She busted out laughing, shaking her head at me. "First get the lipstick off your teeth, Cinderella." She said still laughing.

I turned to face the mirror. My front tooth was just as red as my lips. "I," I hesitated. "I was just saving that for later." I shrugged. We laughed together.

"Right."

We left the house and headed to meet the guys. I was nervous, excited, and I really couldn't wait. My first real date, or double date I should say. Let's do this.

free

16

Jackson

I heard girls giggling in the hallway and figured Kennedy was home from a drunken night out.

When I glanced at my alarm clock it read 11:27 pm. That was an awful early night for her.

Tucking my arm back under my pillow, I closed my eyes to tried hard to fall back asleep. It was no use though. I already wasn't sleeping well, and the noise was driving me crazy.

I sat up in my bed and ran my fingers through my hair. Switching on the lamp, I reached for my shorts and pulled them on. It had been a rough week for me. Coach was pushing us extra hard during our workouts and with school being so hectic I just couldn't keep it together. The pressure was over-whelming me. Not to mention I only had two more semesters before graduation. I was majoring in Sports Science, and minoring in sports management. Coaching was what I always intended to do, but now that it's almost here I'm scared to death. What if I couldn't find a job, or what if I hated it? I had discussed these things with my advisor at school and she recommended me taking a couple of classes that would allow me to focus on other things. Once the semester started I realized that I probably wasn't cut out to do anything that didn't revolve around sports. It was too difficult for me. There was nothing that I wanted more than to be involved in sports. It's just scary to think about what life would be like after graduation, and even scarier when I think about my grades and whether or not I'll actually graduate.

I let out a deep sigh and padded my way out the door.

Food was what I needed.

When I walked into the kitchen I was surprised by what I saw. The noisemakers had made their way into the kitchen. But that wasn't what surprised me. Standing there in a long white nightgown was Grace, beautiful Grace.

"Sorry Jack, were we being loud?" I heard Kennedy ask, but my eyes weren't looking at her.

"It's okay." I replied still looking at Grace.

"Hey Jackson," she said with a small smile. Her long blonde hair hung in curls around her face, and her lips.

Jesus.

Her lips were stained red. She was wearing lipstick.

As if I didn't already picture her lips doing dirty things, it'd be worse now.

I was supposed to be forgetting all about her. I was supposed to not allow her in my thoughts at all. There was no way in hell I could keep her out now. This was serious. My body was fighting me all the way, because I wanted her right then just as much as ever.

"Where'd you go tonight?" I asked Kennedy after I finally unglued my eyes from Grace.

"We had a double date."

My eyes snapped back to Grace.

"You both had a date tonight?"

Grace shifted on her feet and I wished I could read her mind.

"Yes. Both of us." Kennedy replied. "Shit, I have to check my email. I was supposed to hear back from my professor. I'll be right back Grace."

I could feel all of the air leave the room as soon as Kennedy left, and in a flash, Grace was leaving too. She was rushing to get away from me.

"Goodnight Jackson," she said as she moved around me.

I don't know why I stopped her, but I did. I grabbed her hand, and she turned back around to face me. Her chest was moving fast with each breath she took. I pulled her closer to me, and watched as she swallowed heavily.

"What are you doing to me?" My voice was low and breathless. My heart was racing. I'd never felt like that before. Never. It wasn't supposed to be this way. It was supposed to be easier, but nothing with Grace was easy.

"I don't know what you're talking about, I didn't do anything to you."

Oh naïve girl. If you only knew what you did to me.

Every inch of my body wanted to be near her, including my heart, and I had no fucking clue why. My mind said, "don't do it."

With my free hand, I reached up and touched her face. I slowly ran my thumb along her soft bottom lip. She sucked in a deep breath that was so loud people in the other room could hear it. Good thing no one was around.

I didn't move though. I touched the corner of her mouth and stared into her eyes.

I was mad at her.

I was angry.

Who the fuck was I kidding? It was never her I was mad at. I was mad at myself, for treating her like shit.

I inched my lips in, closer to her face. It was an agonizing pace. "I want to kiss you Grace. I want to kiss you so bad." I whispered.

"What are you doing to me Jackson?" She stunned me with my own question.

"Making things right."

"For you or for me?" She asked and I could see the worry behind her eyes. I knew what she was asking of me. And the answer wasn't the right one. It wasn't the one she wanted to hear. I wanted to kiss her because I was selfish and I wanted it, and it wasn't fair to her. I didn't think I'd be able take whatever this was between us any further, at least not outside these walls. Not now. Hell, maybe she didn't want anything from me. Maybe this was one-sided. Maybe she didn't want me near her at all. I'm no mind reader, but all the signs were there. She was attracted to me. That was clear, but that was all I knew. All I knew for sure anyway.

I pulled back from her. I couldn't do it. I couldn't lead her on. She was too sweet, and too pure. I'd already proved to her what an ass I was. No need to make it worse.

"What are you doing?" She asked.

"Making things right, I told you." Only this time I really was.

"What if?" She started to ask something but hesitated. I thought she was going to try again, but the look on her face was strange. She was afraid to say it, or confused.

"Just say it Grace."

She opened her mouth, but snapped it closed hastily.

"Say it." I pushed.

"What if I want you to kiss me?" Her lips were moving so quickly that I barely caught what she said. Her eyes dropped down to the ground.

"You do?" I asked playfully. I wasn't stupid. I knew she wanted me to kiss her. I could see it all over her. The attraction was there.

"Don't make me say that again?" She smacked my chest.

Her innocence was truly the prettiest thing about her. It was like it glowed around her and made her brighter, and more beautiful.

"You're so damn cute." I admitted.

She blushed and looked up at me through her long dark lashes.

"I can't kiss you." I said, and a horrified look came over her face. "Don't do that. Don't think that this has anything to do with you, because it doesn't. I want to kiss you. I want to kiss you bad, but for all the wrong reasons.

I'd just be leading you on. I'd be pretending that this was something that would lead to something more, and it wouldn't. I can't."

She started to reply but Kennedy interrupted. Grace took two swift steps back away from me when she heard Kennedy's footsteps approaching. Her back was flush against the wall and her eyes were glued to the floor.

"I got an email from my professor and she agreed to meet with me, but she wants me to meet her super early in the morning. I'm sorry Grace. I hate to make you get up early, but I don't have a choice. Looks like I'll be taking you home at the crack of dawn in the morning."

"That's no problem. I'm used to getting up early."

"This is really early. We would have to be up by five." Kennedy explained.

Grace laughed. "Seriously it's not that early. I'll get up."

"I'll take you home." I said. I wanted to.

"No, that's okay." She said, without even so much as a glance in my direction.

"I'll take you home Grace." I was more serious this time, and wasn't about to take no for an answer.

Kennedy spoke up for her. "That'd be great brother. Then little Gracie here can get her beauty sleep.

Grace rolled her eyes. "Stop calling me that." She giggled and so did Kennedy. I was lost, but sweet Grace was back.

"I don't have to leave until ten." I said.

"Okay." Grace replied.

"Goodnight." I said as I walked away and left the girls standing in the kitchen.

I walked into the bedroom and closed the door behind me. I threw myself onto my bed and groaned into my pillow. She was knocking all my damn screws loose. Every last one of them had come undone. I couldn't function around her. I closed my eyes tight, and willed the sleep to come.

Please come.

free

17

Grace

I heard Kennedy get up and leave this morning, but I didn't open my eyes to let her know that I was awake. I had been lying there for the last two hours careful not to stir and wake her. Sleep was painfully hard after my encounter with Jackson in the kitchen last night. I'd grown impossibly brave next to him. I had wanted him to kiss me so bad, but he didn't. I pretended that I was okay with it, but I wasn't. It only confirmed what I already knew. He didn't want to be seen with me, or lead me to believe that he wanted something more. I'd have to try and find away to erase him from my head.

That was a task that I was clearly going to lose at.

I could have easily told Kennedy I was awake and let her drive me home, but instead I laid there in the bed pretending to sleep so that I could ride with Jackson. Sheesh. This was already ugly.

There was a light tap on the bedroom door and when I glanced at the clock it said 7:00 a.m. Some one else was up too. I smiled just thinking about Jackson being on the other side of the door. Then I wanted to kick myself for smiling.

I opened the door just as Jackson was walking away.

"I'm sorry. Did I wake you up?" He asked.

I shook my head no.

"I made some breakfast if you want something to eat."

"You cooked?" I asked. I was shocked.

"Don't get too excited. It's scrambled eggs and toast. And if the toast happens to be a little dark and crunchy, and the eggs are a little rubbery, well don't blame me." He smiled.

Wait, did he say eggs? My eyes were so focused on his bare chest that my ears didn't even register that he was speaking.

"Did you say eggs?"

He laughed and rubbed his chest. Clearly I'd been caught. He was the hottest thing I'd seen in person besides that Liam guy that was on the cover of one of those fru fru magazines that were at my local grocery store back home.

"Keep that up, and we won't make it too the kitchen." He turned around and walked away leaving me standing there with my mouth hung open. My feet were planted and I couldn't move. Nope. No moving. They suddenly felt like they weighed a hundred pounds apiece. Why did he say things like that? I had a love hate relationship with that mouth of his, more of love, love relationship actually. I loved what came out of it, the way it moved, the way his breath felt against my face, and the way his bottom lip was so much fuller than the top one. Good grief.

It was just words Grace. Take a deep breath and pull yourself together.

"I'm just teasing Grace." He called out from the end of the hallway.

The breath that I didn't even realize I was holding came barreling out. He had never been that open with me before, granted his mouth got away from him at times. Even though it was the boldest thing a guy had ever said to me, I still liked it. I liked it way too much.

We ate our rubbery eggs in silence for the first five minutes. I barely even looked up, too frightened that I'd get embarrassed from his earlier confessions.

"If you want to get dressed, I can take you home when we're done." Jackson finally broke the silence.

"Okay." I sat my fork down. The house was so quiet. "Where are your parents?" I asked. I hadn't seen them and was hoping I'd get to meet them.

"My dad works a lot, but when he's not working they take a lot of trips. My mom goes with him on work trips too." He explained.

"That sounds nice. They must get a long great."

"Yeah. It's kind of disgusting actually." He said, scrunching up his perfect nose.

I rolled my eyes. He must find that the act of love a disgusting thing. Not me though.

"What about your parents?" He asked.

"What about them?" I stood up from the table and carried my plate to the sink.

He stared at me from across the room. "I don't know. Do you talk to them? Do they work? You never say much about them."

"No, I don't talk to them much. My dad is a farmer, and my mom is a housewife. She stayed home and homeschooled me and my brother." I explained.

"Why don't you talk to them?"

I eyed him from the sink. "It's complicated." That was as much detail as I cared to give.

"Were you always homeschooled?"

"Yep," I replied.

"Wow, that's crazy. I couldn't imagine being homeschooled."

"It wasn't too bad."

"I don't believe you," he said as he walked over and stood beside me in front of the sink. "No friends, and no sports." He shook his head. "I would've been miserable."

"Yeah, you wouldn't have lasted a week." I exaggerated. But it was probably the truth. I couldn't begin to imagine what he would be like if he didn't have sports or his popularity. "I'm going to go change and then I'll be ready to go. Thanks for breakfast."

"You're welcome. I feel bad that you actually swallowed it."

"If I come down with some horrible virus then I will've learned my lesson."

"Ye of so little faith." He held his hand against his chest above his heart. Gosh, he was adorable.

"Get dressed, would ya?" I stomped off smiling.

I am Free

We pulled up in front of the house and my heart dropped to my feet. There, parked against the curb was my fathers green pick up truck. I knew it was his. The same bumper sticker that had been on the back bumper for years was still there.

What was he doing there? Was he coming to get me?

"Please keep going." I cried out.

"What?"

"Don't stop Jackson, please." I fought to catch my breath. I didn't want to go back home. I couldn't go back. I just couldn't.

"Where do you want to go?" He asked frantically. He had no idea what was going on.

"Drop me off anywhere. I don't care. Just not there." I pleaded.

"What's wrong Grace?"

"Just drive." I pleaded.

I rocked back and forth in the seat, trying to calm myself down. I don't know why I was getting so worked up. He couldn't make me go. Or could he? The power he had over me was great. I knew that I'd be relentless against his words.

I was eighteen years old. I was legally old enough to leave, but he had such a hold on me. He held all the control over my life and I couldn't stand it. All I wanted was to be free, and he wasn't going to let that happen. I couldn't stand up to him. I'd break down into a million little pieces, and he would see to it that the power was all his.

Poor Aunt Darcy. What was he saying to her? Would he hurt her? I tried my best to calm down, but I felt like I was about to hyperventilate.

We pulled up into a parking lot on the campus at the college and he turned off the ignition. My mind was racing, filling with crazy thoughts of what my father might say or do. That scared feeling I used to get when I was near him was overtaking me. I was back to being eleven years old. Back to being the child that my father scolded every chance he could. I'd hoped that I'd never have to feel that way again, but I was wrong.

"Start talking, because you're freaking me out." Jackson said as he turned to face me. He reached for my hand and held inside of his.

"Can I use your phone?" I asked.

He pulled the phone off the charger, pushed a couple of buttons, and handed it to me. "Just dial the number and then hit the green button." He said.

I dialed Aunt Darcy's home phone and waited for her to pick up.

"Hello." She answered.

"Aunt Darcy, it's me."

There was a short pause. "Vicki, it's so nice to hear from you." What? I was confused. Who was Vicki?

"No, it's Grace." I said.

"Yes, Vicki, how are you?" She said the name again.

Suddenly it clicked; she didn't want my father to know that it was me on the other end of the line.

"I drove by the house and I know that dad is there."

"Yes, yes, that's right." She said in a cheerful tone.

"I'll be back later when he is gone." I said, rushing the conversation.

"That sounds great."

"I'm so sorry Aunt Darcy." I nearly broke down into tears.

"Oh no dear, don't you worry about it. I'll get those papers for you as soon as I can."

She was a great actress. Even I believed her, and I was on the other end of her performance.

"See you later."

"You have a good day too Vicki. I'll talk to you soon. Bye, bye," she said as she hung up the phone.

"Why can't you see your dad?" Jackson spoke up again as soon as I handed him the phone. He wasn't going to let it go.

"I don't want to talk about it Jackson." I opened the door and climbed out. I was going to spend the rest of the day walking if I had to, anything to keep from having to go back there and see him.

"Oh no you don't." He rushed after me. "You owe me a little more explanation than that. I'm worried about you. Whatever happened back there," he said as he pointed to his car. "It scared me. I was worried."

I stopped walking and looked up at him. There were deep wrinkles on his forehead where he was frowning at me. There was definitely worry in his eyes, and I had to tell him something.

"I ran away." I blurted out.

He cocked his head to the side. "Aren't you eighteen?" He asked.

I nodded. "I am, but I left my parents in the middle of the night. They had no idea I was leaving. I caught the first bus here, and I've been staying with my aunt."

"It's not running away when you're eighteen. It's moving out."

I sighed. "I told you it's complicated. Now please don't make me talk about it anymore." I begged.

"Okay, I won't, but I'm not going to let you just walk around like your lost or something. Come on. Get back into the car and we'll go somewhere."

I didn't have the strength or will to argue. He was right. I had no idea about this part of town and I really didn't want to be wandering the streets alone. I caved easily. Walking back to the car, I climbed in and started to fasten my seatbelt. He leaned in the driver's side door and gave me a curious glance.

"Do you just want to go someplace quiet?" He asked. His clear blue eyes stared directly at me. Quiet sounded like the best idea in the world.

"That'd be great."

"Then unbuckle your seat belt and come with me."

My eyes squinted in his direction for a moment, but I did as he said. I stepped out of the car and walked next to him as he led me around the side of a building. We walked in step for a little bit. I had no idea where he was taking me, but I didn't care. All I knew was that no one was around, and the quiet walk was enough to ease me.

He led me across a long field of grass and up to a chain link fence. It was the back of a baseball field, a very large baseball field. I assumed that we were still on the campus, but there wasn't a sole around. He sat down on a patch of grass and leaned his back up against the fence. Then patted the ground next to him for me to join. I gave him a small smile than plopped down beside him. Literally I plopped, as if the weight of the world was on my shoulders.

It wasn't really. There were people who had it a lot worse than I did, than I ever did, people who would probably give anything to have my life. I was being childish, but I was holding out hope that once he couldn't find me, that he'd stop looking. That he'd finally leave me be, once he realized I was never coming home. I wanted to stop having nightmares. I wanted to never think about home being anywhere but Aunt Darcy's.

Silly, I know. But I could still hope.

I'm not quite sure how long we had been sitting there, but the day seemed to pass by quickly. I was lost in thought thinking about my dad, and how much rage he was probably carrying for me. He couldn't take me away. I loved it here. I didn't want to go. I'm sure people that ran away from their homes probably did everything imaginable, like scary unmentionable things.

I didn't.

That wasn't me. It wasn't the kind of person that I was. I didn't want to be free because I wanted more. I wanted to be free because I wanted less. Less hurt, less abuse, less guilt, and most of all less heartache.

I felt Jackson's hand grab hold of mine and snap me out of the daze that I was in. He squeezed it gently. I glanced up at him through hooded eyes. "You hungry?" He asked.

"What time is?"

"Just past four o'clock."

"In the afternoon." I looked at him in shock. Had we been sitting here that long?

He let out a soft laugh before replying, "It's certainly not four in the morning."

I let him pull on my hand to help lift me from the ground. "Wait, didn't you have some place you had to be?"

"Yeah," he tugged me to him, and wrapped his arms tightly around me. "Right here." He said.

The scent of him was all around me. It was like a blanket that I never wanted to let go of. He smelled so good. I wrapped my arms around his waist and fisted my hands in his shirt. I rested my head against his lower chest and breathed him in. It felt safe, so safe that I didn't want to let go of him. Not ever. I was the girl who felt unfamiliar in a hug, not the girl who enjoyed one, but he was different.

"Grace." He spoke softly.

I lifted my head up but kept my body close to him.

He slowly moved his head down to towards me. My body trembled beneath him. My lips were shaking and my heart was racing. This was it. He was going to kiss me. Could I breathe? I wasn't sure. My world stopped. Every inch closer that he moved made my heart skip a beat. His eyes shifted from my eyes down to my lips, and then back up again. I wanted that kiss so bad.

Please kiss me Jackson. I repeated inside my head.

The heat between us was intense. It was breathtaking. He stopped just short of my lips and looked at me deeply. I thought maybe he was waiting for me to say that it was okay, so I smiled just barely. He closed the gap in an instant, pressing his soft, warm lips to mine.

I don't know where my heart went but it felt like it was taking flight from my chest. So soft and gentle, he moved his lips slowly over mine. It was so much better than I expected. A hundred times better.

The electric current flowing through my body was unlike any feeling I'd ever had before. It consumed me. I kissed him back harder because I couldn't get enough of him. I wanted to stay like that forever. I figured the deeper that I pressed into him, the more real it would feel. Wrong. It made me feel like I was floating on a cloud and that every part of my body was under a hot, steady, stream of water.

I felt the tip of his tongue press against my lips.

Once.

Twice.

Three times.

That was when I realized that I was supposed to open my mouth. When I did, he slipped his tongue gently inside of mine. Forget what I said earlier. This was the moment that my heart took flight in my chest. The tingles were all the way to my toes. It didn't get better than that. It couldn't. I never knew that it could feel that way, and that I'd want to be this close to someone.

A sound came from him that made me weak in the knees. He loved it too. It triggered something deep inside me. I clenched the back of his shirt and pulled myself to him with all the force I had. I kissed him back as if he were the last person in the world. I kissed him as if I needed him to breathe.

My breath was gone. My heart was gone, every plausible thought in my mind, gone.

When ours lips shifted apart, he held me up. I needed that. My knees were weak and my legs unsteady. If I tried to stand there on my own, I'd be a goner. I'd fall straight to the ground.

There was a bright smile on his face.

"That was amazing." He said.

"The best first kiss ever." I admitted. It just slipped out, but I didn't care.

"First kiss?" His head dropped to the side. "That was your first kiss? I was your first kiss?"

I could feel the heat in my face. Embarrassing moments were my thing. "Well, technically it was my second kiss. If you count the one you gave me on my cheek."

"That's hot." He brushed his lips against mine for a second, than pulled back a little. "Damn that's hot."

I giggled into his chest.

"Let's go get food." I said.

"Let's go." He took me by the hand and walked me back to my car.

I wasn't sure what had changed. He was acting so different. I didn't know what had gotten into him, but I couldn't escape the feelings that were taking over inside me. They were strong. I didn't know Jackson that well, but I couldn't deny what was happening. Something was happening, and it made me happy. It made me forget all of the worries that were waiting for me at home.

I read about these kinds of feelings before in century old tales and stories. When you have no television, books become your best friend. Well, books and radio. But reading about it, and feeling it were two completely different things. My parents weren't like that. They didn't show their feelings, so this was all so new to me.

I could get used to those lips on mine.

Seriously, I could.

18

Jackson

I didn't want to leave Grace at her Aunt's house after what had happened earlier, but I had to get to weight training. She told me it was okay. Her father wasn't there. So I left her, but not without a goodbye kiss. I was sinking myself in deeper and deeper with her, to the point that it scared me.

I'd never been kissed like that. There was so much feeling and she was the most delicate girl I'd ever touched. She was like a piece of forbidden fruit. Then when she admitted that it was her first kiss, I almost lost it. It was the hottest thing ever, but at the same time it brought me back to the thoughts of her innocence. How the two of us were worlds apart? She was good, like goodie two shoes good. I decided that at weight training I would feel out the guys about her. Just see what they thought and if any of them could see past her differences.

It was a bad idea all around, because the moment I mentioned her they started with the jokes. They made fun of her. They called her plain Jane, even made jokes about how she was as pure as holy water. Hell, I even laughed at that one.

My thoughts were all over the place. I couldn't figure out one side from the next, and with basketball about to start full swing I just couldn't afford the distractions. Not from anyone.

Even Holly.

Fourteen new texts today, and all of them were from her. She was becoming unbearable, and I couldn't take it.

As soon as training was over, and I'd gotten back to my car I called her. Of course she answered on the first ring.

"Where have you been all day? I tried to call you several times." She nagged. It took her two point five seconds to start in on me.

"We need to talk."

"About what?" She asked. "About how you never call me back, or how you don't answer a single one of my texts."

I growled and slammed my hand down on the steering wheel. I was going to ask to go over to her house and talk, but fuck that shit. I couldn't handle her whining and her bitching and complaining.

"I want to break up." I said. Just like that. I was over it.

"You are not serious Jackson. Quit acting like this, I'm the best thing that has ever happened to you." She yapped in the highest voice possible.

I wanted to scream back at her, but I didn't. I just bit my tongue and let her rant and rave for five minutes.

"Are you done? I have to get home, and I am not arguing with you. I told you I want to break up and I'm serious. I can barely keep up with school and basketball. I don't have time for a relationship." I admitted, and that was the truth. Well, part of the truth.

"You'll regret this."

Ha, that wasn't happening. "I don't think so. Bye Holly." I hung up the phone and threw it into the seat, but not before putting it on silent. I had a bad feeling that she would keep calling back until I answered and I wasn't in the mood.

I needed to be all work and no play now. The season was starting and I didn't have time for the drama. No matter how much Grace was on my mind, I couldn't let her get me off track either. For some reason I kept finding myself being pulled in her direction. Most of the time I felt completely helpless when my mind would wander to her. It had to stop.

I would just keep telling myself that, even though I knew it was a big fat lie.

Now after that kiss, I'd have to work double overtime to keep her out of my head. Maybe it was because secretly I really wanted her there.

19

Grace

I was nervous about going back into Aunt Darcy's. I was afraid that my dad would be lurking somewhere in the shadows waiting to scold me for being the world's worst child. Followed by a long truck ride back home to my nightmarish childhood.

I found Darcy in the kitchen drinking coffee at the table. She looked frazzled and tired. It had surely been a long day for her. Five minutes with my father would have made for a long day.

"Hey," she spoke as I walked into the room.

I pulled out the chair across the table from her and sat down.

"Hey." I said in a low sad voice. "I'm so sorry."

"Oh no honey. There is no need for you to be sorry. That man is a hard ass all on his own. You don't have to make excuses for him."

"I know, but it's all my fault that he came. I should have never run away from home the way I did."

"Technically you didn't run away Grace. You're eighteen years old. You were free to leave home at anytime. You didn't need his permission. I have to know though," she paused and reached her hand over to touch mine. "What really happened? Please tell me, because I have a feeling that it was bad. I need to know."

Was I ready to talk about?

Absolutely not, but I knew that I had to. She has been nothing but good to me. I owed her that much. I just wondered if she was really ready to hear the details. This was her brother, and though she despised him, I wasn't sure if she could really handle the truth.

I took a deep breath and looked to her for comfort. I wouldn't tell her everything just the most important thing.

"There was one really bad time. I don't like to talk about it, but I will for you." I swallowed the lump in my throat. "You know that he's strict, and you know that he's mean. The one time that has stuck with me is when he beat me in the shed and left me there bleeding."

Aunt Darcy sucked in a hard breath, as the tears streamed down her face.

"I was caught in very little clothing, when the girl next door to us ran off with my clothes while I was swimming. He didn't like that my skin was showing, and he wanted to make sure that I never did it again." The words came out of my mouth so fast. It was like someone had knocked the breath right out of me.

"My God Grace." She shook her head. "How old were you?"

"Fifteen," I replied.

She wiped her fingers under her eyes and shook her head. "How bad?"

I gave her a confused look.

"How bad was the beating?" She asked.

I stood up and turned around where my back was facing her. I un-tucked the shirt from inside my skirt and with both hands I raised it up. The scars were visible to her.

"You have to be fucking kidding me right now." She yelled out. I heard the chair scoot out from the table as she came around to get a closer look. "This is not okay Grace." She cried out.

I felt her arms rest on my shoulders, and her body began to shake. Her head came to rest on my back and the sobs came tumbling out of her. It shook my whole body as she cried, and I couldn't find the strength to keep it together. I cried too.

I don't know why. I thought that I'd already cried enough over this, but her tears brought out my tears.

I turned around to face her and she pulled me in for the tightest hug. "I'm so sorry. God I'm sorry." She said over and over. Her words only made me cry harder. "You won't ever go back to that. Do you hear me?"

All I could do was nod. There was no way I could get the words out, if I tried.

"You are eighteen years old, and you don't have to go back with him. I will not let you go back. It was wrong what he did. It was evil." There was anger in her words. Not towards me, but towards my father. He deserved the anger, because he was mean and cruel.

We stayed locked in each other's arms and continued to cry until there were no more tears left. Then we spent the rest of the night on the couch with a bucket of ice cream and the worst/best reality T.V. marathons that we could find.

I am Free

Two weeks had passed since my father came to town. The phone calls didn't stop though. He called many times and yelled at Darcy. I felt horribly guilty for the pain that he was causing her. I knew that it was my fault. He wouldn't stop until he found me, but I couldn't bear to face him yet. Strong or not, I had just trudged up the past with Aunt Darcy, and I knew that facing him would break me completely.

Kennedy had been calling and stopping by as often as she could to check on me. She changed her schedule around at the library so that the two of us would have more shifts together. It was nice. She did everything she could to keep my mind off of the situation, including a slumber party at my house with hours of T.V. I loved her even more for it.

Jackson on the other hand had somehow caught the plague. It was the only explanation I could give myself for the reason he never called or came by. I never saw him at the library either. He'd fallen off the face of the earth or got sucked in the black hole. Maybe basketball was taking all of his time, or maybe he truly didn't want to see me. Either way, I didn't like the way it made me feel. I thought the two of us were going to be a lot closer after our day spent on the campus or after the kiss we shared. Guess I was wrong?

I guess leopards can't change their spots.

I will cross off being played in my little book, and try and move forward. There were too many things for me to be grateful for.

Who was I kidding? I wouldn't be able to get Jackson or that kiss out of my mind no matter how hard I tried.

Every poem that had been written since our kiss had been about him. I had the lovesick blues bad. I wouldn't tell Kennedy that though.

After my long shift at work, I came home to find a message on the table.

Grace,

I'm gone to Paul's and won't be home tonight, but you can call me anytime on my cell if you need me. There is some cash in the jar on top of the microwave if you need it, and left overs in the refrigerator. Call me for ANYTHING! Also, a guy named Preston called for you. He sounded cute. Make sure you call him back.

Love you,

Darcy

I laughed at her note.

Under her scribbled handwriting was Preston's phone number and a smiley face. I wondered what he wanted. I hadn't spoken to him in a while. Our last date or double date I should say went really good. He was so nice.

I picked up the phone and dialed his number.

"Hello," his voice came over the line.

"Hey Preston it's Grace."

"Grace," I could hear a smile in his voice. "I'm so glad that you called me back. I've been so busy lately and I'm sorry I haven't called sooner."

"That's okay. What's up?" I asked and smirked. As soon as those words left my mouth, I knew that I sounded just like Kennedy.

"I was hoping that the two of us could get together tonight for dinner. If you want?" He asked.

"Ugh," I stuttered over my words. "Just the two of us?"

I could hear a faint laughter from him through the phone. I must have sounded like a complete idiot.

"I was kind of hoping it would just be the two of us."

I sat there for a moment not saying anything. This would be a real date. Not that the others weren't real, but this would be different. The word "alone" was flashing through my head like a Las Vegas street sign.

"Oh, uh." I struggled.

"Unless you don't want to." He said quickly.

"No, I do. I'm sorry. I'd love to." I replied, trying to hide the nerves from my voice.

"Good, okay. I'll pick you up at seven?"

"Sure, that sounds good."

"See you then."

"Bye."

I hung up the phone.

Holy moly. I was going on a date. Alone. In one hour.

I picked up the phone and dialed Kennedy as fast as my fingers could dial.

As soon as she answered I cut her off instantly.

"No time for small talk Mrs. President. I have a date with Preston in one hour. Alone."

"Shit, no way."

"Yes way." I nodded my head even though she couldn't see me through the phone.

She laughed loudly into my ear. "Well sister, you're on your own on this one. I can't come and lend a hand because I am buried under a pile of homework. Besides you don't need me. Wear that light blue skirt and the cute white top that Darcy got you, and don't forget your lipstick."

"What am I going to say? What will he talk about? What if he wants things from me, like romance kind of things?" All of my words slurred together.

"Grace! Calm down. It's okay. You don't have to do anything that you don't want to do. That's the good thing about having a vagina."

"Don't say vagina." I replied.

"Well I'm not calling it a monkey. I refuse."

178

I sighed. She was insatiable.

"Just be yourself and have fun." She said.

"Okay, but be ready for a long phone conversation when it's over."

"I'm here for you babe."

"I better go get ready." I sounded far from enthused.

"Have fun." She said and the line went dead.

The nerves had set in and I was not at all ready for this date. I hoped that our conversations would be as easy as before, not complicated because we were alone. I didn't want there to be awkwardness between the two of us. Preston seemed like a really nice guy. I mean, he's no Jackson, but I can't compare the two. They are night and day. One guy likes me and wants to spend actual time with me, while the other is on the fence. One day Jackson likes me, and the next day he doesn't. I can't make him want to see me or spend time with me, especially when I have someone else who really does want to spend time with me.

There had to be no more Jackson nonsense.

I rushed up the stairs to get ready for my date.

I took Kennedy's advice and put on my light blue skirt. It only took me about twenty minutes to get ready, so I had to sit for thirty minutes on the couch with butterflies in my stomach. So many thoughts were running through my mind.

Would he be a gentleman? He had been so far.

Would he want more from me? I had no idea.

There were so many unanswered questions. I wondered if this is what all girls went through before a date. I was going to give myself an ulcer just thinking about it.

The knock on the door couldn't have come at a better time.

I peeked out the side glass to make sure it was him, and it was. Opening the door, I found Preston standing there with a small bouquet of flowers. He looked so cute and sweet standing there. I instantly felt much better.

"You look great." He said as he handed me the flowers.

"Thank you." I opened the door wider. "Come in." I smelled the fresh flowers for a moment. It was very thoughtful. "I'll just take these to the kitchen, then we can go."

He waited patiently for me in the living room. His bright smile lit up the place. It made me smile too. I liked the way he felt so comfortable around me. It made such a difference. His confidence was one of the things I liked most about him. He was never ashamed to be seen with me. It was nice.

"I'm ready," I said once I realized that I had stood there far too long staring at him. He hadn't noticed that I was, thank goodness.

Once we were inside his car, I finally asked where we were going.

"I thought we'd have dinner, and then we could just take a walk if you want." He answered as he pulled away from the curb.

"That sounds nice."

We chatted lightly all the way to dinner. He was so easy to talk to. I don't know why I had gotten myself all worked up. It was all for nothing. He could easily lead a conversation and I never felt uneasy. Even the silence wasn't awkward.

The only thing that bothered me was that in those few moments of silence, my mind wandered back to Jackson. No matter how hard I tried to keep him out, he was always there.

Those lips.

Those eyes.

I wondered if for one single moment he thought of me too.

20

Jackson

It's our last night of freedom before basketball season starts full force. One last hooray and we usually did it up right. I planned on drinking until I didn't know my name, or Grace's.

Yep, she was still on my mind, every fucking minute of every fucking day.

I thought I could do it, that I could handle whatever was happening between us. I was beyond wrong. It scared the hell out of me. Scared me bad enough to make me run.

Her kiss was like fire and ice. It freaking sucked me in, so bad that I thought I'd die from it. Death from kiss…

Right, like that hasn't been done before.

How about death from shriveled up balls? That sounded more likely.

I was meeting the guys at the bar for a few drinks before we headed to the park. We always ended Freedom Night with a bonfire and music at the park just outside of town. It was a secluded place where we could do just about anything we wanted, and we never got caught.

Reaching on my nightstand I grabbed my cell phone and my keys. The night was young, and I was ready to kick it with my friends. I wanted a drama free, alcohol filled, night of fun.

I met Jeremy at his house, and left my truck parked in his driveway. By the end of the night, I was hoping that I wouldn't remember my name let alone be able to drive. He came out of his front door just as I was making my way on to the porch.

"Hey man. Right on time, you ready to go?" He asked.

I nodded. "It's been a long damn day. I'm ready to blow off some steam."

"You and me both brother."

"Are all the rest of the guys meeting us there?" I hadn't spoke to any of them, so I didn't know what their plans were.

"Yeah, they're probably half lit by now. You talked to Holly?"

I groaned.

"Sorry man, I was just wondering."

"It's not you. I'm just aggravated. I want to drink away the thought of all females tonight."

He laughed as he started the car. "You got it. But just so you know, she'll probably be there tonight."

"Well, I hope I'm drunk by the time she shows up."

He cranked up the stereo as we headed towards the bar. There was no more talk about Holly or any other girls. We wouldn't have a chance to speak anyway with his stereo volume set on max. The car rattled and thumped all the way there.

I rubbed my ears as I stepped out of the car and onto the curb. "I don't know why you have to listen to that crap so loud."

"It's better that way you big baby." He tossed his arm across my shoulder. "Us big boys like our music loud, and our women even louder. If you know what I'm sayin?"

I just shook my head. "I hear you, loud-n-clear."

After a couple of hours at the bar we decided to head down to the park. The bar was too damn crowded, and it took too long to get a drink. Thank goodness we started with the shots. I felt really good. Not drunk but good. We loaded the cars up with as many as we could fit inside and took off.

Pulling onto the gravel driveway that led to the field next to the park, I noticed that there were a lot more cars than usual. We had to park pretty far back, and walk most of the way. The music was loud, and coming from somebody's pickup parked close to the bonfire. The night air was cool, and people were all over. It didn't feel crowded like the bar, and I suddenly wished we had just come here first.

I spotted the keg of beer as we closed in on the crowd of people. I took off in that direction.

"Where you going?" Jeremy hollered.

"To get a beer." I called back over my shoulder.

It was wide open. I filled my cup full, and took a sip when I heard Holly's voice from behind me.

"Jack," she said in a sultry, smooth voice.

It didn't repel me like it normally would. Must have been all the booze. I felt her hand touch my back and move lower as she stepped in front of me.

"I've missed you baby." She whispered into my ear.

I didn't respond, because I knew I hadn't missed her. Except maybe the way she touched me. I may have missed that a little.

She started to say more, so I tipped back the cup and finished it in one drink.

"You want to go someplace quiet?" She purred as she ran her hands along my chest.

It didn't mean that I wanted to get back together. I just craved her touch. There were needs. I had needs.

She linked her finger through the belt loop of my jeans and tugged me forward. I was game. My mind was a bit fuzzy, but I knew what I was doing. I didn't lead her on. I didn't come on to her. But you can't tell a sexy girl no. Not when her touch was so familiar. I was just getting her out of my system.

Fuck it.

Who cared anyway? I didn't

I let her take me, in more ways than one.

21

Grace

"Okay, which one do you like?" Aunt Darcy held up two brightly colored cell phones.

"You really think it's necessary?"

"YES!" Both Darcy and Kennedy said in unison.

Okay.

Both phones looked so expensive, but Aunt Darcy said not to worry. She was putting me on her plan.

"The red one." I smiled and snatched the phone. I was actually really excited, but I didn't want to show it. I didn't want to feel like I was using my aunt, but she was so persistent. It was for my own safety.

"I knew you'd choose that one. You little rebel." Kennedy said nudging my arm.

It was pretty. Red had become my favorite color. It matched my toes, and my lips.

"You have to show me how to use this thing." I said to Kennedy as we walked up to the counter to purchase the phone. "And while we are here, take me to the makeup store. I want some red lipstick." I was feeling a little rebellious, now that she'd mentioned it.

Kennedy started cheering inside the store like a crazy lady, and drawing all kinds of attention. It was hilarious. We were a perfect pair, the two of us.

"Oh, Mom and Dad are home tonight, and she's making a big dinner. She asked if I wanted to invite you over to eat. What do you say? They are dying to meet you."

"That sounds like fun." Darcy chimed in.

It did. I hadn't met her parents yet, because they were rarely home. I wanted to though. Kennedy always talked about them, and they seemed like such great people. Different from what I was used to. I couldn't wait to meet them.

"Sounds great." I said cheerfully.

For hours, Kennedy and I played on my new phone. She showed me all kinds of things. The camera was my favorite though. We must have taken a thousand photos.

Some were goofy, and others were sweet. I never had a camera growing up. I think we may have taken family photos once my whole life, and only one single picture was hung up in our house. My Mom and Dad's wedding photo sat on the mantle in the living room. That was it.

Kennedy drove us to her house just after five o'clock. When we walked inside, I got kind of nervous about seeing Jackson. We hadn't spoken in a while, and I wasn't sure I was ready to see his face. Those beautiful eyes, and that wicked grin, of course I wanted to see him. Who was I kidding? The stupid boy was crowding my brain more often than not. So much so that I hadn't even paid attention to Mr. Black Sheep himself, that stood in the living room.

"Well if it isn't Gracie." Tucker called out from the living room as we were walking through. "You are even more beautiful today." He winked.

I smiled back at him and shook my head. I don't know how he did it. He had to be the most charming human being on the planet. "Thank you." I replied.

"Shouldn't you be home eating your own food Tuck?" Kennedy linked her arm through mine and pulled me into the kitchen. I waved over my shoulder at Tucker because I just couldn't help myself. He was always so sweet to me, and despite what everyone said, I didn't think he was a black sheep.

Resting against the island in the kitchen were Kennedy's parents, both of them. They smiled big as we walked into the room. I instantly smiled back at their warm faces.

"Hey guys," Kennedy spoke first. "This is Grace." The two of them walked over to where we stood. "Grace these are my parents Nick and Claire."

I knew what was coming, and I was prepared. Claire hugged me first. "It's so nice to finally meet you." She said. "Kennedy talks about you all the time. You are just as beautiful as she described."

Wow. That was so sweet. "Thank you. It's nice to meet you too. Thank you for having me for dinner."

"Of course. You're welcome to have dinner with us anytime you like." Her smile stretched across her face. She looked nothing like what I'd pictured. Her long dark hair and wide set eyes were beautiful. I don't think any of the kids looked like her. Except for maybe that smile, they all shared that warm smile.

"Come here sweetheart," I slipped into Nick's arms for a quick hug. Instantly I wondered if I'd ever get used to all the hugs. I had my doubts. He kept hold of my arms as he stepped back to take a look.

"Pretty isn't she." I heard Tucker's voice, and flushed red.

"Don't mind him. I'm glad you could join us. You make yourself at home okay?"

"Yes sir." I replied.

"You call me Nick." He nodded.

"Okay."

There was something about the way that he said "home" that made me feel more comfortable. They really did have a home here. There were two nice parents who loved each other, and kids who adored them. My home wasn't like this, at least not my old home. It was getting better everyday though.

"Supper is ready if you guys want to find a seat in the dining room." Claire said as she kissed Kennedy on the cheek.

"Come on Gracie. You can sit beside me." Tucker said as he pulled me through the kitchen.

Oh Joy!! I was guaranteed to spend the entire meal wearing a red face thanks to Tucker.

The table seated six people. Kennedy's parents sit on each end. Tucker and I sat next to each other, and Kennedy was directly across from me. She and I both sat next to her mom. It didn't go unnoticed that there was an empty seat.

"He's on his way." Tucker whispered in my ear.

I looked at him and quickly at my plate. He'd caught my eyes lingering on the empty chair. Talk about uncomfortable. I tried hard to act like what he said didn't affect me, but it did. He was coming. Jackson would be there any minute.

"Stop worrying your pretty head."

I looked back up at Tucker who was grinning.

"Are you psychic or something?" I asked him in a low voice.

"Nope. You are just so easy to read."

"Shit!" Kennedy had said the same thing to me before. If they could read me so well, then so could Jackson. I must've looked like an idiot in front of them.

All eyes were on me. And it dawned on me, what I had said. I'd cussed, loudly, and in front of everyone at the table. If I weren't embarrassed before then I was now. I slapped my hand over my mouth quickly, and started to apologize. I couldn't believe that I'd done that. I was making a wonderful impression. I hadn't even really cussed in front of Kennedy. Those words were usually left in my head where they belonged.

Tucker started to laugh, and everyone joined in. Even Claire and Nick couldn't hold it together. Laughter filled the room. Once Kennedy joined in, I couldn't help but laugh too. It really was funny. My father would have washed my mouth out with soap and would've beaten me to a pulp. But here they just laughed, and so did I.

"What's so funny?" Jackson said as he locked eyes with me as he walked into the room. He was wearing a jersey, so he must have just gotten out of basketball practice. All the air in my lungs left swiftly. He had that effect on me.

"You missed it Jackson. Little Gracie said the word shit in front of everyone." Kennedy said, and I smiled at her. I still couldn't find any words or any air for that matter.

"Sorry I missed it." Jackson said as he looked at me again.

I wasn't. I was glad he wasn't there to see me make a fool of myself.

Conversation picked up as they discussed basketball, and school. They gave me plenty of time to relax before they asked me any questions. I was grateful. I told them about my Mom, Dad, and brother who were back home, but didn't give any details. I also told them about my plan to attend college as soon as I had saved up the money. They were such genuine people. They listened to me as I spoke. It was lighthearted and nice, and I really enjoyed myself.

I tried my best not to look in Jackson's direction anymore, but I couldn't seem to help myself. My eyes seemed trained in that direction. Luckily Tucker's carefree conversation swayed me at times.

"How old are you Tucker?" I asked.

"Too damn old for you," he replied. "And it sucks."

A small laugh escaped and I glanced again in Jackson's direction. He looked mad. His eyebrows were drawn together in a hard line, but not at me. He was looking right at Tucker. There was some kind of silent conversation going on between the two of them. The more Tucker smiled, the angrier Jackson got. I turned my head, pretending not to notice and joined into the conversation with Claire and Kennedy. They were discussing Kennedy's job at the Library, and I hung onto their every word. I was trying my best not to have my attention appear elsewhere. Something was up between the two of those boys, and I didn't want any part in it. The less I knew, the better.

It only took one meal with Kennedy's parents for me to know that they were amazing people. I had such a great time, despite my awakened feelings for Jackson arriving at dinner.

I offered to help Claire clear the dishes and clean up, but she wouldn't have it. No matter how many times I told her that I didn't mind, she'd say no every time.

I had to be at work first thing the next morning, so I was ready to leave. Aunt Darcy wanted to spend a little time with me before she left on her trip with Paul. He was taking her some place special for Thanksgiving, which was only a few days away. I was thrilled that for a short period of time, she wouldn't have to worry so much about taking care of me. She could spend time with Paul, and focus on her love for him. It seemed that ever since I'd arrived into town, she'd been fussing and worrying about me. That's not how I wanted it to go. I wanted her to pretend that I wasn't there. I wanted her to go about her every day life as if I wasn't intruding. That hadn't happened.

"Thank you so much for having me over for dinner. I really had a great time." I said to Claire as she was wiping the table off in the dining room.

"Oh honey, are you leaving?"

"I have to work in the morning, and Aunt Darcy is leaving on a holiday trip tomorrow night. I wanted to spend a little time with her before she left." I explained.

"How nice. What will you do for Thanksgiving? You can't spend it all alone. You have to come spend it with us. I insist."

"I..." I started to protest, but Claire's eyes were so sincere. "I... I'd love to." I replied.

Claire clapped her hands together in excitement. "We like to host a dinner party, so it's kind of a big thing. You should bring a date?" She winked.

A date?

I hadn't realized that I would need a date. Would Jackson bring his girlfriend? I couldn't be the only person at the party without a date. Or could I? If Kennedy didn't bring someone, then neither would I.

"It's okay dear." She leaned in close. "Sometimes you have to bring other boys, so that you can make that special one jealous." She whispered.

It's funny how well these people knew me that had only just met me. My own family didn't even know me that well.

"Thanks," I hugged her.

"You're welcome. Come back and see us soon."

I nodded, and met Kennedy at the bottom of the steps. She was driving me home. Before we left I poked my head inside the living room where all the guys were watching television.

"Bye guys," I waved.

"Bye Grace. It was great to meet ya." Nick said.

"You too."

"Later Gracie. I miss you already." Tucker called out to me.

"Right," I shook my head and waved.

I didn't wait to see if Jackson said anything. Turning on my heels, I headed straight for the door. It felt good.

I didn't want him thinking that I needed his goodbye. I was just being polite. Besides, I didn't owe him anything. Not after his retreat from me. He should be lucky I even spoke to him at all.

Ugh… Even my thoughts were turning impolite. It made me feel gross. I needed to go home, write in my book, and shower away the disgusting things in my head.

i am *free*

22

Jackson

We had a scrimmage and two full practices this week. I was exhausted. The last thing that I wanted was to deal with a house full of people. I hated how they turned Thanksgiving into some damn circus. My muscles ached, and my knee was swollen, and all I wanted to do was lay down with an icepack and watch football on the T.V. in my room.

Mom insisted that I join. More like –told me I'd better be there or I was in serious trouble. I wasn't some kid that she could punish, but I'd still do what she said. She was Mom. You don't let her down.

It took me three tries, but I finally got my white tie just right. It lay against my dark gray shirt that was tucked into my slacks. I looked like I was going to prom or something stupid like that. I wasn't the type that wore a tie, only on special occasions or at funerals.

I locked my bedroom door behind me, so that I wouldn't come back upstairs and find some random kids playing with my shit. Coming up the stairs as I was walking down was Tucker.

"Where the fuck is your tie? Why don't you have to wear one?" I fussed. He was even in jeans and Doc Martins. "Not fair."

"You know I never do what I'm supposed to do. I'm the horrible son." He gasped, mocking me.

"You're an ass." I said as I made my way down the steps.

"Maybe I am, but at least my girl isn't here with someone else?" He laughed.

What the hell was he talking about? I didn't even have a girl. The only person he could be talking about was Holly, and she wouldn't dare show up here with someone else. She wasn't even invited.

Rounding the corner into the family room, I spotted Grace. She was wearing a long black skirt, and a white button down top. It was the first time I'd seen her wear black. It was a little tighter too. I could see the curve of her ass, as she turned to the side. It hugged her just right. The top was short sleeve with little ruffles and buttoned all the way up to her neck. She had her long blonde hair braided to the side and that damn red lipstick on her lips.

An angel on earth, she was. I had never seen her look more beautiful. She took my breath away. If anyone else was in the room I would never know it. She lit it up.

A large hand reached for hers and they laced their fingers together. I followed that hand all the way up. It only took one glance at his face for me to feel like someone threw a brick at me. Forget the pain in my knee, the one in my gut hurt way worse.

This was what Tucker meant.

Fuck this shit.

She can't just walk up into my house with someone else. What kind of an ass hole does that?

I growled.

The kind of person that gets treated like the way I treated her, that's who does that. That makes it suck even worse.

"Grace," I said sternly as I moved in close to her. I didn't pause. I didn't hesitate. I pulled her to me and kissed her cheek.

"Jackson." She said in a surprised voice.

While she was pressed up against me I looked the dude straight in his eyes. There was recognition there. It took me a second, but I finally remembered him from the bar. He didn't look too happy with me, but the feeling was mutual.

She shoved me a little to break from my grip, and looked into my eyes. It wasn't an I'm-glad-to-see-you expression. It was more like a, you're-crossing-the-line face.

She took another step back, and eased herself into his side. "You remember Preston, right?"

How could I forget? "Yeah."

"What was your name?" Preston asked, holding his hand out to me.

"Jack," I informed him. Taking hold of his hand, I gripped it tighter than normal so he'd get a fucking clue.

He squeezed back. If this was a battle of brutes than he was toast.

"Dinner is ready. Let's just head into the dining room." Mom spoke loudly above the roar of the crowd. For special occasions we ate in the formal dining room. The long mahogany table would seat around twenty people. Mom loved hosting parties in there to show it off. She was proud.

Kennedy had her arm linked through some guys. She bounced all the way to the table. I obviously didn't get the, bring a date memo. It was ridiculous. This dinner was going to be the longest, most unbearable dinner ever.

I squinted at the name card on the table, and frowned at Mom. She couldn't be serious. She set me right in between the lovely couples, one girl on each side of me. Mom just smiled when I tried to let her know just how pissed off I was. All I had to do was eat, and then I'd be put out of my misery. I could lock myself in my room for the rest of the night.

Tucker glared at me from across the table. He wore a big cheesy grin on his face. If my foot would've reached him, I'd have shinned him. He was the one that started this whole mess anyway. All that flirting he did with Grace at the dinner table, and calling her Gracie. I didn't need this. I was supposed to be trying to get over her.

No one in this family was trying to help. They didn't realize my struggle. They acted like she hung the God damned moon, but I knew the difference. People thought she was a freak. Granted she'd changed some since the first time I'd met her, but she was still wearing tennis shoes under that skirt. I'd bet my Xbox she was. Those damn white shoes that barely had a sole, the ones that with a few more days of walking to work her toes would break through the fabric.

My shoulders sagged as I slouched in my seat. There was no need in pretending that I wanted to be there. Mom had everyone around the table tell what they were thankful for. It was tradition. Most everyone's answers were the same. They were thankful for family, friends, and good health. My answer was short. I was thankful for my team and my family. Only at the moment, I would've traded some of my family in for zoo animals instead.

Grace surprised me with her answer. She said. "I'm thankful for this family, and my freedom."

I didn't know exactly what she meant. I knew she had issues with her Dad, but to what extent, I had no idea. It was obviously a lot worse then what she had been letting on. I reached my hand over and touched her leg, just above her knee. She flinched, but didn't look in my direction. For some reason I wanted her to know that I was thinking about her. She reached for my hand and pushed it away. I watched Preston link their fingers together on the table. She didn't push him away.

She held it.

She held it tightly.

I couldn't watch this shit.

I stood up from my chair and walked around to Mom. "I'm not feeling well. I'm going to lie down. Save me plate." I kissed her cheek and walked out. Torturing myself wasn't what I'd envisioned for this dinner.

I ripped off my tie, tossing it onto my dresser. Unbuttoned the silky shirt, and left it in the middle of my floor as I climbed into bed. I just wanted to sleep. I wanted to forget that the night had ever happened. I wanted to forget Grace. I wanted things to go back to way they were before she strolled into my life and screwed things up.

Her "I'm thankful for" confession kept replaying in my head over and over.

I slipped on my headphones, and cranked up the music. Can't think about it if you can't hear it right?

Wrong!

23

Grace

I apologized to Preston several times before he pulled out of the driveway. I was staying with Kennedy for a couple of nights, so we said our goodbyes at the door. He said that I had nothing to apologize for. He'd had a great time. It puzzled me when I thought about the night and day differences between Jackson and Preston. Preston was different. Jackson was an immature, spoiled brat.

He made me so angry tonight with his childish display in front of Preston. He would never have done that if he'd been around his group of friends, or anyone in public for that matter.

I sat down on the concrete bench in the front yard. I could feel the coldness through the seat of my dress. What a long night it had been. Preston had given me the sweetest kiss on the cheek before he'd left, but it didn't compare to the heat of Jackson's lips.

It bothered me that I was constantly comparing the two of them. I acted like it was some wrestling match and I was the prize trophy to be won. If only it were that easy. One guy likes me, and one guy likes the thought of me. My blinders needed readjusting.

"What are you thinking in that pretty little head of yours?" Tucker asked as he took the seat next to me. He was a big guy. He nearly took the whole bench.

"I don't know." I sighed. I did know. Just didn't think talking to Tucker would solve my problems.

He draped his arm over my shoulders resting the weight on the back of the bench. "You love him don't ya?"

"No." I answered quickly. I didn't love him, and I was aware of that.

"Not Preston." He looked down at me with his knowing eyes. The stare alone was causing me to fidget. "Come on fess up. It's just me here."

"Maybe. I don't know if it's love. I can't stop thinking about him. I can't get him out of my head."

"He loves you too." Tucker responded matter of fact.

"No he doesn't. He's drawn to me because I'm different. That's all this is. He's so immature. Do you know that he used me to get a good grade on a paper? Then when I said hi to him in public, he acted like he didn't even know me." My shoulders sagged at the thought. Saying it out loud made it sound even more foolish. "Then he kissed me."

The air was thick outside and Tucker didn't respond. He waited for me to finish.

"We shared that moment, and he didn't speak to me after that. It lasted weeks. The other night at dinner was the first time I'd seen or spoken to him since then."

I smoothed down the top of my skirt with my hands waiting for him to speak. I couldn't say anymore. I'd already told him more than I'd even told Kennedy. He was just so easy to talk to.

"You know I've got say something in my brother's defense even though I probably shouldn't. Yes, he can be a complete jackass. But I know that he loves you. He's been raised completely different."

I interrupted. "That's no excuse, look at you. You were nice to me from the moment you met me and so was Kennedy."

"I know. But Kennedy and me, we're not the star of the basketball team. We never cared about popularity or status, at least not me anyway. Kennedy never really cared either I don't think. What I'm trying to say is, Jackson is singular. He's never been good at school. He's always been the center of attention, the star of the team.

Whatever keeps him on top is what he does. It's because he hasn't truly grown up yet. I see a change in him though. He does care about you."

"Just not enough to be seen in public with me."

"Not yet." Tucker scooted a little closer to me on the bench.

I leaned my head over on him. "You think he'll come around."

"I think he loves you too much not too. You are an amazing girl. I know that you've had a rough past. Anyone can see that, but look at you now. You've come out of your shell since the first time I met you. You're definitely not as uptight."

"Hey." I squeezed his side. "Thank you Tucker." I wrapped my arm around his waist and initiated a hug. Me. I did that.

He hugged me back.

"You know that I have a brother back at home." I said. "He would never listen to me like this or even talk to me. It's really kind of you."

"What an ass?" He said, talking about my brother.

"Yeah, what an ass." I replied. We laughed together. He stayed there holding on to me. "You know I'm a pretty good listener, if you ever want to talk to me about your problems."

"I have no problems. I'm master of the universe." He said in a cocky tone.

"Sure, whatever Master."

"Thanks Gracie." He kissed the top of my head.

"I think I'm going to bed. It's been a long day, and I'm tired." I admitted as I stood up from the bench. The grass was cool against my bare toes. "Goodnight."

"Goodnight Gracie."

I carried my shoes as I walked inside the house. Kennedy's date was still there and she was cozied up with him on the sofa in the living room. The room was still filled with people. Saying my goodnights, I endured my round of hugs before heading to Kennedy's room to go to sleep. Before I could close my eyes, I knew that I had to write. The talk with Tucker was still fresh in my mind. It would help to get a few feelings down in my book.

I changed into my nightgown and crawled into the bed. I switched the bedside lamp on to give me a little light to write by. When I was back at home I used to use a tiny little candle to write by. My dad would throw a fit if we left the lights on past a certain hour. It was too petty of a fight for me to disobey him.

Three Hearts

One to love

One I love

i am **free**

One I am

Two make sense

Two feel right

Two will fit

Three will love

Three will learn

Three's a crowd

I love one

But there are two

Together we make three!

Three hearts

Three hearts

Three hearts

I'm not sure why I included Preston in my poetry. Maybe it was because he was so good to me. He was sweet and sincere. He held my hand on the table today for everyone to see. He didn't try to hide his affections. But I'd be lying to myself if I said that I had feelings for him. I didn't. One childish, immature, jealous, and overbearing jerk held my heart.

As I lay there in the bed, I wondered what my life would have been like if I'd stayed. I'd probably be dating some farmer who sucked up to my Father, and wouldn't care about me at all. He'd probably want to follow right in his footsteps. Take over the farm one day, and raise a house full of kids.

Kids.

I wasn't sure I ever even wanted to have kids. It was too late at night to be thinking about that. I tucked my notebook under my pillow for the night and drifted off to sleep.

24

Jackson

"Wake the hell up."

I felt my body shake again with force. When I opened my eyes I saw Kennedy sitting on my bed.

"What time is it?" I asked.

"I don't know. Just past midnight or something."

"Get out of my room." I growled at her.

She didn't listen. She scooted herself back against the headboard. "No. We have to talk."

"No, we don't" I accentuated the word we. I was dreaming, and she screwed it all up. "Get out." I tried shoving her off the bed.

"Stop Jack. I want to talk about Grace."

I rolled over onto my back, and sighed heavily. "This conversation can wait until morning."

"You love her don't you?" Kennedy blurted out.

"I'm not having this talk with you. You've got five seconds to get the hell out of my room. I'm not kidding."

"For once in your freaking life, you and I are going to talk. She's my best friend. Something is going on. I want to know. She's had a bad life you know?"

I didn't know. We'd never really discussed her life at home. "No I don't know. I don't know much about her life before she moved here. What do you know?"

"Very little. I think she'll talk to me about it someday, but I get the feeling it was real bad. Actually, I know it was real bad. But despite all that, she is still the greatest girl I've ever known. She doesn't care about what people think, and she wears her heart on her sleeve." Kennedy paused a moment. "I don't know if you're trying to play with her emotions or what, but it has to stop. You can't pretend to like her when no one's looking, and then love her behind closed doors. It doesn't work that way. I used to look up to you. I used to think that I would kill to be as popular as you are. I was there once, and I admit that it was because of you that I was. But she made me see the light. She made me realize just how stupid we were. Grace is the type of person who always sees the good in people no matter how they treat her, or what they look like. We should be taking a page from her book."

I swallowed my pride at Kennedy's words. She was right. I knew it all along. I knew that I was toying with her because I was embarrassed. I didn't want to be with her in public, but I didn't want anyone else having her either. So she was different. She wasn't that different. She was simple. God, what have I been doing? I'm an asshole.

"You are such a jerk. I can't believe that she'd even consider having feelings for you. Hell, I'd rather see her with Tucker than with you." Kennedy said.

"I am jerk, but don't say that. It pisses me off."

"Good," she stood up from the bed. "Get pissed off. If you love that girl, than you'd better start fighting for her, because if you don't then someone else is going to steal her heart right out from under you. And frankly, I hope that happens."

She was angry. She was so mad at me, but I could understand why.

"I get it." I said.

"Do you? Do you really get it?"

"Yes, damn it." I ran my hands down my face and sat up in the bed.

"Do you love her?" She asked, but I didn't reply. "Do you love her?" She yelled this time.

214

"Yes." My admission surprised me. I did love her; I just hadn't admitted it to myself. I was young, playing basketball, trying to get an education. This was the type of thing that I'd been avoiding. For some reason it didn't seem right. I was avoiding her for all the wrong reasons, when I should have loved her for all the right ones.

"I knew you did. Stop being arrogant okay. Show her you care, and treat her like you care too."

"She loves you too." I heard Tucker say from the doorway.

"And how do you know that?" I asked.

Tucker came into the room and plopped himself down on the bed. This was the first time since we were kids that were all in the same room alone, just talking.

"She told me Brother. I had a long talk with her outside today. I think she's mad at herself for loving you, because she feels betrayed. She feels like she's wasted her time having feelings for someone who doesn't have them in return." He explained.

Kennedy laughed.

"What's so funny?" I asked.

"Tucker is the voice of reason. I never thought I'd see the day." She laughed again.

I laughed too. She was right.

"Hey now. You two are the ones who thought I was the black sheep. You just never gave me a chance. Like I told Gracie, I'm master of the universe. I can't help it if you two idiots never saw it before. I'm King of the World."

"Good God. Get out of my room before your large head suffocates us all." I said, rolling my eyes. "I get what you guys are saying, and I'm going to do better. Maybe it just took a little heart to heart with you guys to see it. I'm requesting that we don't ever do this again though. Stay out of my love life, and out of my room."

"He's back." Tucker and Kennedy said in unison.

"Damn straight. Now get out." I pointed towards the door.

25

Grace

It was fun spending the weekend at Kennedy's, but I was glad to be back home. I wasn't glad about the 15 messages on the machine from my angry father, but glad that I could get back to my day-to-day routine. The break off from the Library was nice, but I loved it there. I was ready to get back to work.

Aunt Darcy had a great getaway with Paul. She couldn't wait to tell me all about it when she got home. She shared her stories, and I shared mine over ice cream and Christmas movies. Who knew they showed Christmas movies on television when December hadn't even got there yet?

I laced up my shoes, and grabbed a heavy jacket for my walk this morning. Aunt Darcy said that she'd drive me, but I left her sleeping. I was perfectly fine with walking to work. It wasn't that far. The morning walk always did me some good.

Waiting on my porch as I closed the front door behind me was Jackson. He was standing there with his back rested against the wooden beam, and his hands were tucked deep inside his jean pockets.

"What are you doing here?" I asked. I was confused. He never just showed up at my house before. I was certainly missing something.

"I have an early practice this morning so I thought I'd offer you a ride to work before I go." He replied. I could barely see his blue eyes that were hidden beneath his baseball cap. He looked so good in a hat.

"That's really nice of you. I don't mind the walk though." I really didn't. The walks gave me time to think.

"I know you don't, but I'd like to take you today if that's okay." He stepped closer to me, and held out his hand.

What was this all about? He was like a bucket of ice on a steaming hot summer day. He was freezing cold one minute, and warm and melted the next. Of course I couldn't resist him though. I slid my hand into his, and let him lead me down the steps.

"Thank you." I said.

"You're welcome."

For the first time in a while, I saw a genuine smile. The one that first made me want to kiss him.

Not much was said on the car ride to work. I was still trying to wrap my head around why he was suddenly being so nice. He pulled the car up as close as he could to the entrance.

"Have a good day at work." He said, as I was just about to open my door.

I remember my Mom telling me once that crazy, unmentionable things happened when there was a full moon. I couldn't see the moon at this hour, but I was certain that it had to be as full as it could get today.

"Thank you, and thanks for the ride." I smiled, closing the door behind me. I didn't stay and ask him why he was acting so strange. My Momma did teach me to leave well enough alone.

His kindness didn't go unnoticed though. In fact, I thought about it for the greater part of my workday. I thought about it too much actually. Every time the door opened to the Library I pictured him walking through the doors. It was a hindrance more than anything.

Just before my shift ended I received a text from Preston. He'd been so nice about Thanksgiving. He never once worried about Jackson. He never stooped to his level. He truly was a nice guy, too nice sometimes. His message was sweet, and he asked if I'd call him when I got home from work. This was it. I could no longer trudge along his feelings. I had to tell him that I had feelings for Jackson. No matter how silly and immature he acted, my heart was only with him. It would surely be the most difficult adult conversation that I would ever have, but I couldn't let him continue believing that I had feelings for him when I didn't. It wasn't fair.

It was still light outside when I got off work. It was nice to not have to lock up for a change. I enjoyed being able to get off early enough that I could walk home in the daylight. The sun was deceiving though. The cold chill of the air made my legs cold. One thing about skirts in the winter was that they offered very little warmth. Thank goodness for tall socks.

I took the steps two at a time as I made my way down to the sidewalk. I pulled my hood up over my head to block the cold from my face as best as I could. The temperature had dropped a lot since when I'd gotten to work this morning.

"Grace," I heard someone call after me.

I had already begun walking in the direction of my house. When I turned around I saw Jackson steadily walking towards me.

"Wait up," he called out.

"What…" I started to say, but waited for him to get closer. "What are you doing here?" I asked with a sniffle. The cold was already making my nose run. I wished I had worn my stockings and my gloves.

"I came to pick you, and take you home." "Why are you doing this?" I asked.

"Look, we can talk about it in the car. It's freezing out today. Come on." He turned around and walked in the direction of his car, not giving me a chance to refuse.

I took a seat in the passenger side of the car and rubbed my hands along the top of my thighs. My legs were so cold. He turned the dial of the heat on full blast just before he drove away from the curb. I still had no explanation for his erratic behavior.

"What's going on Jackson?" My voice was barely above a whisper.

"I'm trying, that's what's going on."

That still explained nothing.

"Trying what?" I don't know how I got to be so brave. I think a little bit of Tucker was coming out of me. His quick wit kept me on my toes.

He looked at me with his gorgeous blue eyes, then back to the road. Then back at me. What was he trying to tell me? He reached his arm over to me and placed his hand over top of my hands. One of his hands nearly covered both of mine. His thumbed moved softly over my skin. Just the feel of him made my insides dance. If he only knew what he did to me.

I could have pulled away. I could have told him not to touch me, but I didn't. I craved his touch more than anything. That night at Thanksgiving when he touched my leg under the table, I had to fight everything inside me to push his hand away. The only thing that helped me was the anger. The fact that he could touch me where no one was looking instead of in plain view for everyone to see made me so mad. Even now, in the car, didn't prove a thing.

Still, I didn't want him to stop touching me.

"If you give me a chance, which I know I don't deserve, I'm going to prove to you that I can do this."

What was I supposed to say to that? I wanted to say, yes! "Jackson, I don't know. I mean you barely know me. You don't even want to be seen with me."

"All I can do is apologize for that. You don't have to say anything today. Just give me a chance to prove it to you." He pleaded. I wanted to believe him. I really did. Deep down in my heart I wanted him to change so badly, or to at least feel for me the way I felt for him. "You don't have to say anything. Just don't. I'm going to make you see."

He gave my hand a little squeeze as he parked the car in front of my sidewalk.

"If I call you tonight, will you answer?" He asked.

"Yes." I said, probably with too much enthusiasm.

"Good. I'll call you later." He leaned across the seat and gently kissed my cheek. I closed my eyes when his lips touched me. I wanted to freeze time at that exact moment.

"Bye." I spoke quietly as I climbed out of the car.

Would he call me? I didn't know, but I was going to hold on to the idea that he was. Maybe he could change. Maybe he didn't have to change, he just had to open up. Either way I wanted to be the girl that he opened up for.

My heart wanted him.

26

Jackson

I had my phone in my hand ready to dial her number. I'd been thinking about this call since the moment I left her house. I couldn't wait to hear her voice, and I'd planned on keeping her up for her first all night conversation. I intended to find out as much as I could about her, if she'd let me.

Making myself comfortable in my bed, I pressed the call button. She answered on the second ring.

"Hello." She said hesitantly.

"Hi." I said.

"Who is this?" She asked.

I sat there a minute. Did she not recognize my voice? I knew I'd never actually called her phone before, but I thought she was expecting my call.

"I'm just kidding." She giggled. She really giggled. It was the cutest sound ever.

"You little jokester."

"I'm sorry. I couldn't help myself." Her admission was adorable.

"It's a good thing I can take a joke." I smiled although she couldn't see me. "What are you doing?"

"I was just writing in my poetry journal."

"You like poetry?" I asked. Let the questions begin.

"I love it. I'm not a professional or anything. It's just something I like doing. It's better than a diary to me. More therapeutic," she explained. "Do you keep a journal or anything?"

I laughed. "No. Isn't that a girl thing?"

"No, you jerk face."

"Did you just call me a jerk face?"

"Maybe..." There was that giggle again. "Jackson can I ask you a question? I mean will you answer me honestly?"

"Sure." I was a little nervous, but I'd be honest with her. I owed her that much.

There was a little pause, and I was thinking that maybe she wasn't going to ask after all.

"What made you change your mind?"

"About what?" I asked.

"Me. You were all -I like you let me kiss you, then you were all -I don't want to talk to you or be seen with you. I'm getting whip lash."

I knew I needed to be honest. "Preston." I sighed, "If I'm being honest. I hated seeing him with you. I hated it so bad. I didn't want him touching you. I didn't want him to share whatever thoughts you had in your head. I wanted them to be for me."

She was silent, eerily silent.

"I told you I'd be honest."

"Thank you." The line fell silent once more, but she finally spoke. "Does that mean that this is just a jealousy thing? Do you just want me, because someone else does?"

"No. It doesn't. It means that I'm staking claim on what's mine. Or what I'd like to be mine. I want to be with you Grace. I want to kiss you. I want to talk to you all the time. I want you to be my girl. Not just sometime, all the time." I admitted. I wanted her to know where I stood. I was ready to take that leap with her.

"Your girl?"

"My girl." I repeated.

"Can we take things slow? I'm not ready to turn over my heart just yet." Her voice was low and solemn.

That was not exactly a –yes I want to be your girl, but I'd take it. "We can go as slow as you want? Would you come to my game on Friday?"

"I'll think about it." She said.

Whew. This was going to be harder than I thought. It was just a basketball game. When she said slow, she meant it.

The topic of conversation took a wide left turn and I was glad. We had the serious stuff taken care of. I wanted to ask her more questions about herself. She was always open and honest with me about everything, even when I asked about our kiss. She was not as shy over the phone as she was in person. She was braver. I felt like I could ask almost anything. Almost…

When she started yawning, she said she needed to get off the phone. It was just past eleven, and I could hear just how tired she was. I didn't want to let her go just yet. I persuaded her not to hang up. I used my soft, gravely voice to convince her to stay. Told her that I just wanted to hear her breathing, and it was the truth. I'd never been in a relationship like this. Not one where I wanted to hear her voice, and see her face. Not one where I thought about her all the time. This was so much more. She had situated herself right inside my chest, where I'd break if I ever let her go.

i am free

Her breathing was heavy, and as she drifted off to sleep I could hear a tiny little snore. It was so quiet, that I'd miss it if I weren't really listening. Hanging on the line just a little longer, I waited for her to make a sound, any sound. Did she talk in her sleep? I had to hang up. She wasn't the type of girl that would like for me to be listening to her without her knowledge. She was good and pure, and as innocent as they come. No matter how badly I wanted to lie there and listen to her all night, I couldn't.

I whispered goodnight, and hung up the phone. Breathing deeply and thinking about her beautiful voice, I drifted off to sleep. With her on my mind, I knew I'd have the best dreams ever.

27

Grace

"Grace! Kennedy is here."

"Okay. Be right down." I called downstairs to Aunt Darcy.

At the bottom of the steps Kennedy was waiting. "You ready?" She asked.

"Where we going?"

"Jackson said he invited you to the game, and I'm here to make sure that you go. Mom and Dad are in the car. They're going too."

"I... Maybe..." I hesitated. I was going to kill him for telling her. The point was to take things slow. I didn't want to jump right into things without knowing for sure that he was serious.

"Get your coat and your mittens. Move it sister."

There was no arguing with her, but I gave her an evil look. That would teach her.

"I'm so glad that you decided to come dear. Jackson has been talking about you for days. I'm so glad that you too are finally going to be together." Claire said as she reached around the seat and patted my knee.

Whoa. What? Hold the phone?

Crap. Even in my head I sounded like Kennedy.

I smiled. That was it, and it wasn't even a real smile. It was more like an I'm-truly-frightened-and-I-may-puke, half smile. What happened to taking it slow? Did he tell his parents everything? I hadn't even talked to Kennedy about this, but after looking at her face, she obviously thought this was the greatest thing in the world. Her wide smile spread all the way to the tips of her eyes, and once again I thought I was going to puke.

I turned my head to stare out the window. It suddenly felt like there wasn't enough air in the car. Everyone in it was sucking up too much of my oxygen.

Share. Share the freaking oxygen people.

Nick drove around the parking lot at the school several times, until he finally chose a spot. Claire kept nagging at him to pick a spot some time in this century.

They were highly amusing. I was thankful for their light banter, because it was helping to keep my mind off the inevitable. I bundled up my coat a little tighter, and pressed myself into Kennedy's side as we made our way inside.

The seating was ridiculous at the school. I'd never saw so many people. It was unbelievable the amount of space and people it took to fill up the place. The place was huge. Everyone was wearing their school shirts in support of the team, and I was in my usual skirt and sweater. Sticking out like a sore thumb was something I mastered. There was no need in changing things now.

Nick and Claire led us to our seats, the most amazing seats in the house. They had to be. We were just a few rows from the floor. We'd probably be able to smell the sweat from the players.

I cringed at my thought.

Behind us were thousands of seats, and they rose high up to the ceiling. I could feel my knees tremble at the thought of having to sit up at the top.

"Isn't this amazing?" Kennedy leaned over to speak to me. The packed house was noisy so I could barely hear her.

I nodded my head in agreement. This was my first time. My first live sporting event, my first time inside of an arena that big, and my first time watching Jackson play ball. My heart was beating clean out of my chest.

i am free

Kennedy must have read my mind. She gave my hand a squeeze and then passed the time away trying to teach me about basketball. More like scream at me about basketball. I knew what basketball was; I just didn't know the rules. Kennedy never minded though. She kept right on yelling in my ear. She'd already taught me so much in the time I'd known her, and not just about basketball. She never laughed at me when I didn't understand things, or when I was lost. There was the occasional time when she couldn't help but laugh, but those were the times when I laughed too, right along with her. It wasn't at my expense. Her laughter was never at my expense.

"Don't look now, but Holly is in the building." Kennedy said.

Of course I had to look. I couldn't miss her with her bleach-blonde hair, as Kennedy called it. Her eyes were wide, and I could feel her anger from my seat. She was much better at the evil face then I was. She obviously wasn't thrilled that I was the one sitting with Kennedy and her family. Can't say I blame her. If I were in her shoes, I'd be mad too.

"That's the student section," Kennedy explained. It was a large group of seats just off to the right from where we were sitting. I could fly a paper airplane to them. That's how close they were. "Don't pay any attention to her."

As Kennedy was talking, the lights dimmed. Loud music erupted from the speakers, and the crowd started to chant. I couldn't understand what they were saying, but I was getting eager. A man came over the intercom and announced the teams and the flashing lights went crazy. They were like laser beams through the crowd.

Kennedy reached for my hand, and pulled me to my feet as they were announcing Jackson's team. I hadn't even seen them come in, and they were already huddled around in front of us. It was a sea of red jerseys. They must have come in while I was watching the light show.

"What number is he?" I asked when I realized that I had no idea. "Never mind." I'd recognize those blue eyes anywhere. He must have known where we'd be sitting, because his eyes fell directly on us. His family probably sat in the same seats every time.

He smiled at me as he stood there in his uniform. His jersey had a big number 21 on the front. Gosh, he looked amazing. I couldn't stop staring. His arms were big and meaty. That was the only word I could think of. I thought that maybe I'd need my heart restarted when he winked at me.

I couldn't believe that he did it, but then I realized that no one would have noticed in this stir-crazy room. I was wrong. Glancing to my left, all eyes were on me. Both his parents and Kennedy wore huge smiles on their faces. My face grew red, and we all laughed.

Way to make me embarrassed Jackson. It's a good thing he wasn't close enough for me to touch. I probably would have went for the smack in the back of the head the way my Mom used to do my brother when he was too loud at the dinner table. I stored that away for later; sure he'd give me another reason to use it.

They announced the players' names, and when it was Jackson's turn I cheered along. I couldn't help myself. It was so easy to get sucked into the enthusiasm of the crowd.

I found out rather quickly that Jackson was good. He was very good. I hardly knew anything of the game, but his shots always went into the basket. The game was a blowout win at 72-37.

"What did you think?" Nick asked me as we were walking back to the car. His heavy arm was draped over my shoulder.

I was still wound up from the game. "It was incredible. I loved it. I've never seen so many people before, and I didn't know that Jackson was so good." I rambled on. If I was feeling this ecstatic, I couldn't imagine what it must've felt like to be out there on the floor playing. It had to be a pure adrenaline rush.

"He is good." He squeezed my shoulder tighter. "I'm glad you had fun Gracie."

Oh no.

I looked up at him. "Not you too. Tucker is rubbing off on everyone."

He chuckled.

"You staying the night with me Grace?" Kennedy asked. "I have to work tomorrow too, so I can drive us."

"Sure, why not." I didn't have any other plans.

I took my cell phone out of my jacket pocket and noticed that I had a new voicemail message. I hadn't even heard my phone ring with all the commotion at the game.

I held the phone up to my ear and listened to the message.

"Grace, it's Aunt Darcy. I don't want you to worry, but your father called tonight. He said your Momma is sick. I don't know what's wrong with her, or even if he's telling the truth. You know how that man can be. I just wanted you to know. Call me back when you get this message."

My heart had sunk to my feet. My Momma was sick. Or was she?

I ran my sweaty palms down my skirt, and dialed Darcy back.

"Grace." She answered quickly.

I could feel the tears welling up in my eyes. I didn't want to cry in the backseat of this car. "What's going on?" I asked. The car was quiet and I knew they could hear me.

"I don't know. He called and was acting like a fool on the phone. He demanded that I let you speak with him.

I kept telling him that I didn't know where you were, but he kept insisting. When I wouldn't budge, he told me that your Momma's sick. I don't know if it's the truth or if he's lying. I wanted you to know." She urged.

"What should I do? What if he's telling the truth?" The tears started to fall. I didn't want her to be sick. I loved my Mom, despite our differences. She would always be my Mother. What if she needed me?

"I don't know baby girl. Maybe you should call home." She suggested.

"Then he will know that you're lying. He'll know that you told me." I tried to say in a hushed voice, but speaking through my tears was hard.

"Where are you?" She asked.

"I'm with Kennedy and her parents. I'm on my way to their house to stay."

"Good okay. Just sleep on it tonight. What ever you decide to do is fine. I'm here for you."

"Thanks Darcy. I love you." I said. I'm not sure that I'd ever said those words directly to someone before. If I had, it'd been a long time ago.

"I love you too." She answered immediately.

Kennedy pulled me close to her and hugged me. I just cried as silently as I could.

When I pulled away. I realized that we were already parked in her garage, and her parents were no longer in the car. I never even heard them get out.

"What's going on? Do you want to talk about it?"

I shrugged, but I knew I was going to have to tell her sooner or later. "Can I take a hot shower, and then I'll tell you everything."

She rubbed the side of my arm. "Of course. Come on."

After my hot shower, I put back on the clothes that I'd worn to the game. Kennedy would gladly let me borrow nightclothes, but the closest thing she had to a nightgown was far too short for my liking.

Walking out of the bathroom, I found Kennedy, Jackson, and Tucker all lounged on the bed. Every pair of eyes was glued to me. Let the insecurities begin.

"Don't you have a home of your own?" I asked Tucker, and the room erupted in laughter. Thankfully.

"Don't you?" He teased back.

"Touché." I smiled and joined the rest of the committee on the bed. "Good game tonight." I spoke softly to Jackson.

"I'm glad you came." He took my hand. No one seemed to notice or to even care.

"I told the guys that you were ready to talk to me about some things and I thought they might want to hear to, but if you just want to talk to me then I understand." She looked at me with fear in her eyes. Maybe she thought I'd be angry with her, but I wasn't.

"Okay." I said. "You three are the closest thing to family I've ever had." Telling them shouldn't be hard, but it would be. These kinds of things were meant to stay locked up inside. Going through it once was bad. Reliving it again would be much worse.

"You don't have to tell us everything, but we're here to listen." Kennedy said. She was sincere.

Time to get the show on the road.

"I was on the phone earlier with Aunt Darcy. She said that my Dad called looking for me again. Darcy told him that she didn't know where I was, and she still hadn't seen me. It's the same lie every time. Only this time, he told her that my Momma was sick." I shifted in my seat.

"Should you call home?" Tucker asked.

"That's the problem. I don't know if he's lying, and if he is then he'll know that Aunt Darcy told me. He'll know that I've been with her this whole time." I explained.

"But you're eighteen. There's nothing he can do." Kennedy said.

I've had to explain this so many times. Everyone thought that being eighteen-equaled freedom. In my world even twenty would be a prison. "I know it's difficult for you all to understand, but he still has this unbelievable hold over me. It's hard to explain, but it feels like there is the imaginary rope linking me to them back home. I can't seem to cut it, and it haunts me all the time. Almost feels like I'm strangling to break free." I looked down at my twisted fingers. I was trying to avoid eye contact at all cost. I didn't need to see the hurt expressions on their faces. It would only make things harder for me to explain.

"Are you afraid of him?" Kennedy asked. It was the first time that I'd noticed how silent Jackson was being. He hadn't said anything yet.

"I have been my whole life." I admitted. "Growing up at my house was nothing like growing up in yours, like what you have here."

"Why are you afraid of him?" She asked.

"Why don't you ask me what you really want to know?" I looked at her seriously. I knew that she was skirting all the way around the subject of my back. She wanted to know what happened.

"Did he do it to you?" She asked with certainty.

"Do what?" Jackson finally added his two cents, letting me know that he hadn't completely tuned me out.

"Yes." I answered. "He hurt me, bad, and a lot."

"The fuck." Jackson said, followed by the rants of Tucker. "What did he do?" He asked me.

"He's always been strict and mean. There was a strict set of rules that I had to follow my whole life. It wasn't awful, but confining. I did what I had to do. I waited out the years I had to wait, and then the first chance I got, I ran away."

Kennedy was shaking her head. "Your back… He did that didn't he?"

"Yes."

"My God." She sucked in a hard breath and clasped her hand over her mouth. "I knew it." She admitted.

"I don't want to talk about that day though, okay? I don't ever want to talk about that."

"Just tell me what gave you the scars? Please," she pleaded. I guess it was important to her to have all the pieces of my jagged puzzle.

"A rake."

My blank stare ahead was all I had. There were no tears, and my heart was practically void of all emotion. I already suffered through it, long before this day. I'd already shed all the tears I could. I'd been angry, and afraid, and alone. I was done with all emotions attached to that day.

I found the look on Jackson's face frightening.

"You should call him Gracie." Tucker insisted.

"I'm scared." I felt helpless. I was back to being that little girl running scared from her dad.

"We are all here for you. He can't hurt you through the phone."

Having them there with me would help, but I'd be risking everything. It would be the same as if I just went back home. He'd know where I was, and he'd come for me.

"I need to think about it." I held tightly to Jackson's hand. "I'll decide what I'm going to do tomorrow. I want to talk to Aunt Darcy too. If I call him then he'll be showing up at her house. I just gotta think."

"Why are you so happy?" Jackson said as if that was a normal question. It confused me.

"What kind of question is that?"

"Look at you." His free hand measured me up. "You seem completely oblivious. Since the day I've met you, you've been nothing but happy. How are you not broken?"

I let out a pent up breath. "You forget Jackson. I've had to deal with this my whole life. I've been angry. I've been upset. I've cried plenty of times. This is not me hiding behind my smile. It's real. I have nothing to be upset about. I have a great life. No, I don't have all the same luxuries that you guys have, but I've never had those anyway. I'm proud of myself for being so strong. I'm happy with who I am. Nothing about this life is bad. Absolutely nothing," I reassured him with a smile. "If I dwell on the bad things then I'd be too unhappy to focus on the good things. I hate that I am going to have to face my past sooner or later, but when I do I'll get the closure that I need. Until then I'm going to be me. This is me. I have an amazing best friend, a home that I love, and Aunt who loves me so much, a great job, and this family who've taken me in and greeted me with open arms, literally." I laughed.

"And you're an amazing person Gracie. I've said it before and I'll say it again." Tucker dashed me a gorgeous smile. He stood up from the bed walked around to the side I was sitting and kissed the top of my head. "I'm proud of you girl. You have more balls than any grown man."

"Tucker," I gave him a little shove. The word balls made me blush.

"I'm proud of you too, and I'm so glad you're my best friend." Kennedy said, as she pulled me in for a hug. "I'm going to the kitchen to get cake. Come on, you've earned yourself a big piece."

"We'll be right there." Jackson said.

I cocked my head to the side, eyeing him curiously. I thought we were finished. I thought we'd said everything that needed to be side, or I rather.

Everyone shuffled out of the room, and there we were.

Alone.

He took my hand in his, and helped me stand up from the bed. When his hands reached out to touch the sides of my face, I closed my eyes. I felt his thumbs brush gently against my cheekbones, and down run down the length of my neck. I felt dizzy on my feet. I reached up and gripped his arms with my hands. Opening my eyes, I saw tears. His eyes were filled to the rim with unshed tears. They were so full, that I knew they'd spill over at any moment.

"Jackson." His name barely left my mouth, before he touched his lips to mine.

I nearly fell to pieces under his touch. The tears from his eyes, slid down his cheeks. I knew, because I could feel them too. His kiss was light and better than any we'd shared before. It felt real.

Pulling back I looked deeply into his eyes. "Don't cry for me." I said.

"God I'm so sorry Grace. You're the most amazing person that I've ever known, and you didn't deserve the jacked up life that you were dealt. I've been so horrible." He choked.

"I know I didn't deserve the beatings. But I wouldn't change the way my life turned out. I'm okay with who I am. Really. I'm okay."

He rested his forehead against mine and released a loud breath. I knew that he wanted to say more, but it wasn't going to happen tonight. I just wanted to leave things as they were, to go about the night as if I didn't just spill my guts to them. I needed cake, lots and lots of cake.

28

Jackson

When you are given a great life, you don't realize that other people might not have it so great. Maybe they're living with demons from their past, or maybe they have nightmares because the abuse was so bad.

I'd taken for granted the good life that I'd been given. It was eye opening listening to Grace's story. It brought me to tears to know that she was treated so horribly. She was smart, beautiful, sweet, and so innocent. It was wrong. Life shouldn't be so hard for such an amazing person. It wasn't fair.

When she went home this morning, I couldn't get her out of my head. I thought about her every moment while I was in school, wondering if she was okay, or if she was going to call her Dad. I didn't want her to go through that mess by herself. I kept thinking of how much better it would be if I were there with her, by her side.

I sent her a quick text before class asking her if she was okay, but I still hadn't heard from her. The wait was agonizing, and I grew uneasy with every minute that passed.

If she hadn't texted me back before I left school for the day, then I was going to her house.

"Hey man, you going to The Edge tonight?"

I heard Jeremy's voice above everyone's in the hall, his loud, and obnoxious voice. Stepping to the side, I waited for him to approach me. He would track me down no matter what, so I was just as well to get it over with.

"Don't tell me you forgot?" He said as he dropped his bag to the ground.

I gave him a questionable look. It was true. I had forgotten whatever the hell he was talking about. Too many things were going on. I'd been busy.

"Cory's birthday bash at The Edge. You can't miss it."

"Shit. That's tonight?" I shook my head. "I don't think I can come." I said thinking about Grace. I really wanted to be with her. Who was this person she was turning me into? Never in a million years would I miss one of the guy's birthdays for a girl. But this wasn't just some ordinary girl. This was Grace. My Grace.

"There is nothing more important then this party tonight. Your damn homework can wait. Besides, we're about to have finals and this whole crappy semester will be over. If you ain't passing by now, then you ain't going too."

"Thanks man," I said sarcastically. "Way to punch me in the gut."

"What's gotten into you?" He asked.

"Nothing." I said a bit to hasty.

He shook his head. His long, shaggy hair hung down over his eyes. It was taking over his face. I'd be glad when he cut that shit off, but he wouldn't. Not until we lost a game. He was a superstitious nut. "Whatever man. You don't want to talk to your best friend? I get it. Years and years of friendship obviously mean nothing to you. I thought you loved me man." He joked, faking tears.

"Shut up." I shoved his arm. My phone vibrated from the pocket of my jeans, and I reached in and pulled it quickly. I'd been waiting all day for a message.

I'm fine. Quit worrying would ya? I've decided not to call my Dad, at least not for a little while. Oh, and Kennedy is taking me to The Edge tonight so that I can chill out. Her words not mine.

"So are you going or not?"

"Actually, I think I will." I replied.

"Good, I'll see ya tonight. Text me later if I need to pick you up."

"Yeah okay, see ya." I said, as I replied to Grace's text. A damn tornado could have come rolling through at that moment and I wouldn't have noticed. It's funny how someone so little and plain in everyone else's eyes, could be so strong and beautiful in mine. I wish it hadn't of took so long for me to make her mine.

I told her that I'd see her at the bar tonight, and I couldn't wait. Well kind of. My friends were going to have a field day with this, but I was ready. They could pounce all they wanted, and I wouldn't budge. It was going to be my night to prove to her that I was for real. I didn't want her seeing anyone else tonight, except me.

I am Free

I was on the edge of my stool sitting next to Jeremy when I spotted her across the bar. You couldn't miss her. Her wavy, light blonde hair was the brightest in the room. Kennedy was talking to her and pointing in our direction, and that was when our eyes locked. It was only a brief second before she looked away. Were they not coming to sit with us? I saw her head move back and forth as if to say no. She was looking at Kennedy and not me. They walked a little farther until they were almost at the end of the bar. I could barely see them now through the sea of people. When they were completely out of sight, I'd had enough. I didn't want to wait any longer. Pushing my way through the crowd, I finally spotted them sitting in the stools at the far corner of the bar. I moved in closer, but stopped to look at her before she knew I was there. I had no shame. I could stare at that beautiful girl every day for eternity.

"Jack," Kennedy called out to me. "You leaving the ass-holes to sit with the normal people today?" She asked.

"Nope. You girls are leaving the normal people to come sit with us ass-holes." I grabbed Grace's hand and tried to pull her up from the stool, but she was holding back.

"I don't think so Jackson." She said. Did I mention how much I loved the way she called me Jackson. She never called me Jack like everyone else. Her eyebrows scrunched as she frowned.

"It's fine. No one will say anything." I tried to reassure her.

"That's the problem." She kept a tight grip on my hand pulled me closer.

I shrugged my shoulders. I didn't know what she meant.

"You won't talk to me while we're over there." She said. She looked up at me through her heavy lashes. A sad look was on her face.

"Come on." I nudged her off the stool. It was time to prove my point. She gave me a curious look, and then pleaded with Kennedy to come along.

I kept her hand tucked against shirt as we made our way over to where the guys were sitting.

"Guys!" I addressed the group. "Ya'll remember Grace." A few eyes went wide as they looked at her, but no one said anything. "She's my girlfriend." I announced making sure that my point was crystal clear. I wanted them to know that she was taken, she was mine, and that I didn't give a damn what they thought.

Say what you want guys. You're not breaking me.

Grace looked up at me, but it wasn't quite the face I was expecting. Was she angry? I was trying to prove a point. I just wanted her to see that I wasn't ashamed of her, that I wanted her there with me, around my friends.

Instead of worrying, I flashed her the biggest, funniest smile that I could. And it worked.

She laughed loudly in front of the guys, not caring who saw. It was the greatest laugh, and obviously contagious because some of the guys laughed too. Not all of them, but some.

When Kennedy and Grace went to the bathroom, I told the guys to be nice. One cross word and I'd lay anyone of their asses out. I didn't care. They didn't say much about it, but I knew I'd pissed a few of them off. If they were angry with me then we would settle it later. Not while Grace was there.

She was nearly running when she came back to the table from the bathroom. There was a concerned look on her face.

"I have to go. I'm sorry. Aunt Darcy left for the night, but she just called and said that she didn't know if she locked the door to the house. She's worried. I told her that I would call it a night, and I'd go home to make sure everything was okay."

"Oh, okay. That's fine. I can take you." I offered.

She smiled. "That's sweet, but it's okay. Kennedy said she'd take me."

Oh no. "Let me. Kennedy," I pleaded with my eyes. "I can take her home. You stay for a while." If she couldn't read the eye signals that I was throwing her way then she was blind.

Kennedy paused and gave me a funny smile.

I was going to put her in a headlock when I got home.

"I don't mind Kennedy, if you want to stay." Grace said.

Oh the bad thoughts. They were running crazy in my mind. I had to remember to shut them up when I was with Grace. Don't get me wrong. She was beautiful and my dirty thoughts made for some amazing dreams, but dreams of her body would be as far as I could go. Just dreams. I didn't mind though. I'd wait forever for this girl.

Do you hear me God? I shouted the words in my head. *I'm changed. I'd wait forever for her.*

"Okay." Kennedy replied. "I'll call you tomorrow." She hugged Grace just before we left.

And finally, I was going to get some alone time with my girl, my girlfriend.

29

Grace

Oh boy. What had I gotten myself into? This alone time with Jackson wasn't getting any easier. In fact, it was getting harder and harder for me to control my emotions around him. I could understand the whole forbidden fruit thing now. It was all making sense.

When we'd shared that kiss at his house last night, I questioned all of my thoughts. It was important to me that I wait for sex until marriage. It had never even crossed my mind until Jackson came into my life, and now suddenly it was all I could think of. The curve of his shoulders where his muscles bulged out of his shirt taunted me all the time.

I told myself over and over that my body was a temple. It's something my Mom told me when I was little. She told me never to forget, and I hadn't. Maybe some things about my past were bad, but not everything. I didn't forget where I came from or the good things I'd learned. I wouldn't change either. Not for anyone.

When Jackson and I reached the house and I went to the front door I realized that it was locked. Her whole freak out session was all for nothing. She was probably rushing around like a mad woman, and just thought she'd forgot.

"I'm sorry you had to leave the bar. Darcy sounded really worried on the phone."

He touched my lower back as he led me into the house. Oh, my back. He had to stop touching me. Every time he did, it felt like my body would explode. That couldn't be normal. It couldn't. I had to talk to Aunt Darcy about it soon.

"It's okay. I didn't mind. I'd rather be here with you anyway."

And that right there had me questioning my sanity. He was always saying things like that. It was probably my lack of experience with guys, but certain things that he'd say made me want to kiss his lips. Like at that very moment.

We stood there in the doorway and it felt kind of awkward. I didn't know what to do or say, and feared for the words that would come out of my mouth if I tried.

"Grace," he whispered my name.

"Huh," I replied.

"Can I stay here with you tonight."

Whoa. Ugh. Fear. That was my only thought.

"No. I'm sorry. I didn't mean." He scratched his head and shuffled on his feet. "I didn't mean it like that. Please. Shit!"

My pie hole was still wide open, as Kennedy would say. I didn't know what to say. I could barely look at his adorable face.

"Let me start over." He gripped his fingers around the tops of my arms. It took him a minute to breathe and think about what he wanted to say. I'd never seen him look so flustered. "I just didn't want you to be alone. That's all. With your aunt gone, I thought it might be a good idea if I stayed. Just in case your dad calls or something. I could sleep down here on the couch."

All of his words were slow and steady like he was making sure that he didn't miss a word to confuse me. It was funny actually, the way he talked to me as if I was five years old. If I'd had a newspaper or a magazine I probably would have whopped him over the head with it.

255

i am *free*

Right! Good time to use that swat to the head. I thought.

Without another thought, I swung my hand up and popped him. Not hard, but enough to shake him a bit. It must have been the balls that Tucker mentioned. I was getting gutsier by the days.

"Hey." He stood there stunned. He couldn't believe I'd just done that.

Truthfully, I couldn't believe it either.

I held my lips together tightly to keep from cracking up, but it was too hard. Between his facial expression, and realizing what I'd just done, I couldn't hold it in another minute. We were bent over and laughing our butts off.

"Come on, I need chocolate." I laughed, and grabbed his hand pulling him towards the kitchen. It was bold of me, and I knew it. I never initiated his touch before, but he called me his girlfriend tonight. That's what girlfriends did right? I didn't think anymore about it.

"Sorry I was acting like an idiot." He said as pulled me close in front of the fridge. "You make me do and say funny things. I'm not myself when I'm around you."

"You're wrong." I pushed back the piece of hair that had fallen onto his forehead. "Emotions are real. This is real. I think that this boy or guy, sorry," I smiled. "I think that this guy standing right here in front of me is the real you. It's the person that you're afraid to be. You would never show this kind of emotion in front of your friends, at least not the ones that you're trying to impress. But your real with me."

His head tilted to the side a little, and his eyes were brighter than before. They were so blue that the sky would be jealous. "You amaze me." He said. "Where have you been my whole life?"

Oh, his words. They did me in. I was about to be the boldest me I'd ever been.

Could I?

Oh, I had to. My hands were shaking, and my heart was beating so fast that I thought it might leap right out of my chest.

I looked in his eyes. Then I looked at his lips. He was so beautiful that he took my breath away. Standing a little taller, and a little straighter, I leaned in and pressed my lips against his. I wasn't gentle. I kissed him fiercely, making sure that he knew what his words meant to me. His warm lips against mine eased every possible worry that I could have had. He made me feel wanted.

When I pulled away, he didn't pressure me for more. He didn't take all that he could've possibly gotten from me, and it made me love him even more.

I loved him.

It wasn't the way that I loved Kennedy or Aunt Darcy. It was so much more. This was deeper and beyond my wildest imagination, and I had a very vivid imagination.

In the short amount of time that I'd known Jackson, I'd fallen head over heels in love with him. I thought that it would scare me –this kind of love, but it didn't. The love part didn't scare me at all.

I remember very vividly a quote from William Shakespeare's Hamlet that said, "Doubt thou the stars are fire; Doubt that the sun doth move; Doubt truth to be a liar; But never doubt I love."

I knew without I doubt that I loved Jackson, without one single doubt. Yes, he was the first boy to cross my path, but sometimes God got things right on the first try. At least that was my theory.

30

Jackson

She didn't make me sleep on the couch, but I wished she had. As I lay in the floor next to her bed, I could hear her heavily breathing. Her hand had let go of mine once she'd fallen asleep, but I still held on. I was wide-awake, still thinking about that kiss. I had to be living in some sort of dream world. This was not real. No way in hell this could be real.

My phone buzzed a few times throughout the night, but after reading the first text, I didn't read anymore. The guys were giving me shit about Grace. At least that was what the first text was about. I knew they weren't going to let me off easy about it. What they didn't realize was that I didn't care, not anymore. In a couple of years, we'd all be going separate ways and none of this petty bull crap would matter.

I was daydreaming when I thought I heard someone knock on the door. The second time it sounded like someone was beating down the door. Grace didn't budge. I let go of her hand, and slipped on my tee shirt.

Who the hell would be knocking on the door at this time of night?

The clock by the bed said that it was just past two a.m.

I fumbled my way out of her room and down the stairs where the knocks kept growing louder and louder.

"What?" I yelled as I yanked the door open with too much force. An older man with white hair stood there with a menacing look on his face. His eyes were pure evil as he glared at me.

"I'm here to see my daughter."

Oh, hell no. This was him? This was the man that had beaten my girl. My chest rose in anger as I thought of murdering him with my bare hands.

He walked inside the door through the opening I'd left. "I don't know who you are, but you better get her now." He said.

I was about to protest when he yelled out.

"Grace!"

Please don't come down those steps. I thought to myself.

"You need to leave." I said sternly, but he acted as if I just blended into the wall.

"Grace!" He yelled again.

She stood sleepily at the top of the stairs with a look of terror on her face. She was white as a ghost.

"Dad." She called out.

"Get your stuff. Let's go now." The old man called out.

Screw that. "Don't move a muscle Grace. You're not going anywhere with him." I yelled up the steps. He may have looked mean, but I wasn't scared. If anything he should have been scared of me.

"I don't know who you think you are," he started jabbing his finger in my face.

"I'm her boyfriend, and I'll kill you if you lay one finger on her." I said with as much hatred as I could. I was as serious as a heart attack.

Looked like no one had ever said that to the man, because his face spoke a thousand words. He might have been a tad bit scared of me.

Good.

"Look at you girl." He said to Grace. "Everything I've taught you pushed aside so that you could step out like some cheap whore. You're a disgrace."

I smashed my fist into his face as hard as I could. "Get out. Don't ever come back here again!" I screamed.

When he stood up tall, I thought maybe he'd hit me back, but I was ready. Bring it on, old man.

Grace came trampling down the steps, and stood next to my side. Her hand gripped tightly against my arm. She was afraid, but she didn't have to be. I'd protect her. I'd always protect her.

"Your mother has worried herself sick over you? She's ill Grace. Don't you care at all?"

"I care." She whispered. She cleared her throat. "I care." She said over and over.

"Go! Now!" I screamed. I was over the whole conversation. It ended there, and I dared him with my eyes to say one more word.

He stormed out of the house blistering mad.

I pulled her to the front of me and wrapped my arms around her. She squeezed me back as tight as she could. Placing a soft kiss on the top of her head, I told her everything would be okay.

"Go upstairs and pack a bag. We're going to my house." I told her. "We can talk to my parents, and you won't have to worry about him showing up there."

"O... Okay."

She waited for me to guide her up the stairs. Her hand was still trembling in mine. I wasn't scared, but I was worried about her. I knew that my Mom and Dad would know how to handle this.

My adrenaline was still pumping. I never punched anyone in the face before, especially not someone who was that much older than me. My knuckles were red and would probably be sore the next day, but at that moment I wasn't even thinking about the pain. I wanted to get her out of that house to somewhere where she'd feel safe again.

Once inside the car, I took a minute to finally breathe.

I glanced over at Grace and she was staring blankly out the window. She hadn't said a word about any of it. That scared me most. She should be screaming or crying or something. Not sitting there inattentive and lost. Her knee bounced hard under her dress, and her hands laced together on her lap.

"I'm sorry Grace." That was the only thing I could think to say, and I was sorry. I was sorry for what he said, for how badly she was scared, and for opening that damn door in the first place.

She weakly smiled in my direction. "I'm sorry too."

"For what?" I asked. She had nothing to be sorry for.

"For everything. I'm sorry that my Dad screamed at you. I'm sorry that you had to see him at all. I'm sorry that I fell apart, just like I always do." She was nearly screaming. "I'm sorry that I let everyone down. I'm sorry that you're in the middle of this whole mess. God, I'm just sorry." She cried.

Finally.

I didn't want to see her break down like that, but it's better to see some emotion then nothing at all.

"Come here." I pulled her across the console so that I could hold her tighter. "You don't have to apologize to me for any of that. You didn't let anyone down. So don't say that. Maybe you didn't do things exactly like they wanted you too, but damn it Grace. It's your life, and you should be able to live it exactly how you want to. You're an amazing girl, so don't you dare listen to a single word that he tells you. You hear me?" I said.

She nodded her head against my chest, but she didn't say anything else.

"I love you," I said to her as she held me close. I didn't know if she felt the same way, but for the first time in my life I was in love. I was head over heels for this girl, and knew that I would do anything for her.

She looked up at me with tears running down her face.

"You mean that?" She asked.

"Yes. I do. I love you." I said it again.

"I love you too Jackson."

I knew right then that my world would never be the same. I knew that I loved her so hard that she could break me in a second, and I didn't care.

I kissed her forehead, and both cheeks before finding her lips. "Let's go home." I said.

31

Grace

So many thoughts were running through my head that I couldn't keep them straight, but the one thing that I was most certain about was Jackson. He loved me. He told me so, and I told him that I loved him too.

I sat there on the couch next to Jackson as he held my hand. I let him tell his parents what was going on. Before we even walked inside the house, I'd asked him to do the talking. I told him that he could tell them everything, but I just wasn't in the mood to talk. I was already exhausted. My mind was rattled, and I couldn't bare the thought of saying those words to anyone else again.

Claire came over to the couch to hug me, and for the first time all night I felt at ease. Don't get me wrong,

Jackson was comforting, but there was something different about the love of a mother.

Jackson's father Nick shook his head several times, and I didn't know what he would say. He was angry, in the same way that Jackson was.

"You're welcome to stay with us for as long as you'd like Grace." Claire said as she continued hugging me. I wasn't usually the hugging type, but they were growing on me. And sometimes you just need a hug.

"Thank you." I replied.

Nick walked out of the room, and Jackson followed. I glanced wearily at Claire.

"Don't you worry dear? He's not angry or upset with you. Nick had a bit of an ugly childhood, and I think maybe you remind him of himself." She smiled sincerely.

"I'm sorry." I had the whole apology thing down to an art. I was masterful at it by that point.

"No, no, no. It's fine. I promise. He just needs a minute that's all."

We sat there quietly for a few minutes, and I thought about how much this situation weighed heavily on my heart. I did miss my Mom sometimes, and all though I'd been living happily since I'd left, the scars were always there. Not just the scars that were on my body, but the big ugly ones on my heart.

I couldn't continue to drag everyone into the situation, and I couldn't keep being afraid. I needed closure. Running away made me a happier person, but it didn't make me free.

I wouldn't be free until I said my peace.

I needed to tell them that I was gone for good, and that I was never coming back. I needed to get the rest of my things from that house. I needed to light a match under that final bridge and watch it burn to the ground, so that I'd never have to cross over it again.

"I need to go home." I said loudly as if it were the greatest revelation I'd ever made.

Jackson walked back into the room. "You can stay here for the night, and I'll take you home tomorrow after we get some sleep."

"No." I shook my head. "I need to go back home to Oklahoma."

"What? You can't do that. That's nuts Grace. You can stay here with us as long as you want. Dad even said that you could move in if you wanted to."

What a sweet, sweet family this was.

"I don't want to go home to stay. I just want to go home and get everything off my chest. I want closure. I want my stuff. And I want to tell them that I'll be out of their lives for good." I admitted. "If I don't quit running then they'll never stop chasing."

"We'll take you." Claire rubbed my back. "We will all go with you, and we'll get your things, and we'll keep you safe. If that's what you need to do, then we're here for you."

Jackson frowned, but nodded his head. "If that's what you need to do," he said.

"You all would go with me?"

"Of course we will." Nick said as he appeared from behind Jackson. I didn't even realize that he'd been standing there this whole time.

The large tears streamed down my face.

"We're family." Jackson said as he sat down next to me on the sofa. He took my hand in his and kissed the back of it softly.

Claire's face lit up like a Christmas tree. She was having an unbelievably proud Mommy moment. I saw it on T.V. once. I guess our cat was completely out of the bag, and we couldn't hide the relationship from them. I didn't mind though. If I could belong to any family in the whole world, this one would be it, by a landslide.

"Thank you so much." I wrapped Claire up in another hug.

They were rubbing off on me indeed.

i am free

"I'm going to go call my Aunt. I know it's late, but she will want to know what's going on." I said as I walked out of the room.

I am Free

It was Sunday already, and we were leaving on our epic road trip to freedom. They were Kennedy's words not mine. Aunt Darcy apologized for not coming along, but I knew it would be hard for her. She didn't want to come back to this place either, and I couldn't blame her. She told me she was proud of me though, and we'd talk all about it as soon as I got back.

Yippee.

I rode all the way there in the backseat between Kennedy and Jackson. Both of them exhausted me by trying to keep my mind off of the task at hand. We played games, we sang, we talked, and I was about two minutes from lifting up the back hatch and jumping out. God love them for trying, but my nerves were shot.

When I saw the driveway to my home straight ahead I nearly threw up.

"No more talking please." I said to them as the house came closer and closer into view. I knew what lay in store for me, and the thought made scratching my eyeballs out sound like the best plan of the day.

The car grew eerily silent as we pulled into the driveway. When the car stopped, no one said a word, especially when they saw my Dad walk around from the back of the house.

"That's my Dad." I said to whoever was listening.

"I'd like to have a word with him." Nick said as he practically jumped from the driver's seat.

"Let me out." I told Kennedy, as I pushed her towards the door. I didn't know what Nick was going to do, and this was my fight. I wasn't some little girl anymore and I wanted the power he had over me to be gone.

I could already here the yelling before I reached them. Kennedy was taking her sweet time, and I knew why. She wanted to let her Dad get his say so.

"STOP!" I screamed when I reached them.

I had eighteen years to think of what I'd say to him, and I was drawing the biggest blank. Both men stood there looking at me and waiting for me to say what I'd come to say. Nick nodded his head for me to tell him.

"Dad." I started to speak.

"You come up here bringing these God forsaken strangers into my house to tell me how to raise my children." He started yelling in my face.

"SHUT UP!" I screamed. "I'VE HAD ENOUGH!"

It was the first time in my life I'd ever raised my voice at my father.

I took a deep breath and ran my sweaty hands along my skirt.

"I'm not here to fight, and I'm not here for you to yell at me like I'm this little girl that you have control over. I'm not yours to control anymore. I'm eighteen. I'm sorry that I didn't do everything you wanted me to do, and that I turned out to be what you think is a poor excuse for a daughter. It wasn't my intentions to be disobedient or saddening. I've never done you wrong in my life. I've never deliberately disobeyed you, yet you scolded me as if I were the child of a devil. Well I'm sorry, but this is me. This is the girl that I choose to be, and I don't care if you don't like it. You're just going to have to live with it, because I'm not changing. Not for you, or anyone."

My whole body was shaking at this point, including my voice.

"You came to me several times in my dreams. You were always scary and mean, and I would wake up some nights and pray that you would find the good in your heart, but I'm not sure there is good inside you anywhere."

He started to speak but I held up my hand. He wasn't going to ruin this for me too.

"This family," I pointed to them all standing behind me. "They've shown me more love in the little time that I've known them, then you've showed me my entire life.

You're evil, and one day you're going to pay for what you've done to me." I swallowed the lump in my throat.

"I came back here today to tell you that I never want to see you again. I will get what's left of mine from my room, and I will walk out of that front door. If I ever see your face again it would be too soon. Don't come looking for me. Don't call me. Don't ever show your face at Aunt Darcy's house again. You make me sick."

His eyes were dark and dangerous, but he knew that I meant every word I said.

"One of these days I'm going to get married, and have kids. And when I do, I'm going to love them with every power inside me. I'm never going to hit them the way that you hit me."

"I never touched you." He said.

What?

I was stunned at his words. He was trying to make me out to be a liar, or maybe he truly believed his own lies. Maybe somewhere down inside of him, he'd blocked out those memories because he knew how wrong he really was.

I un-tucked my shirt from my skirt and lifted the back of it up.

I was completely oblivious to everyone behind. I didn't care anymore if they saw, because I knew they'd still love me.

I turned around and let my back show to my father; all the while my true family were shedding tears. When I looked back at my father, his eyes were focused on the ground. He couldn't even face what he'd done.

"Look at me. You did this." I wanted an ounce of sympathy from him, just a tiny little ounce of remorse.

"I'd do it again." He said.

"Go to hell." I said through gritted teeth, but the words had barely left my mouth when Nick lunged at my father. He knocked him onto the ground and started to punch his face over and over.

"Don't ever come near her again!" Nick shouted at my father's limp body on the ground. "Go get your stuff inside, and we'll leave." He told me.

I didn't hesitate. I ran through the back door, but the sight of my mother standing at the stove stopped me. She looked bad, not sick, just tired.

"Mom."

"Grace," she said and came around the stove to see me. That dreadful apron was tied at her waist.

"I'm just getting my things, and I'm leaving." I told her. "I won't be back."

"I know," she said. It looked like she held the weight of the world on her shoulders.

"You could leave too you know." I told her, and I meant it. I wanted her to have freedom like me, but I wasn't sure she'd even want it.

"I'm fine here Grace." She admitted. "I'm glad to know that you are safe and well. Are you staying with Darcy?" She asked but the entire time she was looking over my shoulder as if my father would walk in at any minute.

"Yes. You can call me there if you ever want to talk to me." She probably wouldn't though, but now that she knew where I was, I would know that I did my part.

I waited for a response, but when she didn't give me one I ran off to my old room. There were only a few things that I wanted, and the blanket that my Grandmother made was the most important. I hurried to gather my things, and as I was walking out my door I met my mother. My hands were filled, but it didn't stop her from hugging me. She wrapped her frail arms around my neck and squeezed me. I don't remember the last time my mother hugged me. I dropped everything I was holding to the ground and hugged her back. She didn't speak and neither did I, but we didn't have to. That hug was worth a thousand words.

"Goodbye," I said as I took off for the door. I didn't wait for her to respond, because she probably wouldn't. The tears were flowing so hard out of my eyes that I could barely see anything in front of me.

Jackson and Kennedy met me in the yard and took my things as I climbed into the car. Once everyone was inside, I laid my head down on Jackson's lap and cried.

I cried because I got my closure, I cried because of Momma's hug, I cried because my dad would never change, I cried because I was finally moving on with my life, but most of all I cried because of all of the love I felt around me.

"I love you." I said to everyone in the car; because I wanted them all to know how much they meant to me. I'd never hide my true feelings for them, ever.

Every single person in the car told me they loved me too, and they meant it. I was truly blessed beyond measure.

"I'm free." I laughed, though my eyes were still clouded with tears.

"YEAH!" Kennedy hollered. "Free Bitches."

I laughed and snorted at her words.

"Say it Grace." She gave my leg a little shove.

What the heck?

"FREE BITCHES!" I yelled out and the car erupted into laughter.

So long old life, and hello new, fabulous, one hundred percent, better life.

"I love you Grace." Jackson said into my ear, and kissed my cheek.

"I love you too."

I watched as Oklahoma slowly faded into the distance. Silently, I said a little goodbye. You can take the girl out of Oklahoma, but you can never take the Oklahoma out of the girl.

THE END

Epilogue

Grace

I spent Christmas morning at home with Aunt Darcy, her boyfriend Paul, and Paul's daughter Carly. It was a wonderful morning. Nothing like any other Christmas that I'd ever had. It was the first time I'd met Carly, and we hit it off right away. She was a very sweet girl, just like Darcy had said. I could see the two of us becoming great friends. Both of us girls cried when we watched Paul propose to Darcy right there by the Christmas tree. She said yes of course, and I was thrilled for her. She deserved such wonderful happiness. It got me thinking that maybe I'd need to look for another place to live. Who knew how long it would be before she decided to sell her home. It was something for me to think about anyway.

We continued opening presents for what felt like hours before having a great big breakfast that I helped Aunt Darcy fix. Kennedy showed up just in time to steal a muffin, and to pick me up. I was spending Christmas night at her house with her family. I couldn't wait.

"You should see all the presents under our tree." Kennedy said as we walked up the steps to her house. "Mom said that we had to wait for you to get here before we could open them." She rolled her eyes.

"You guys didn't have to wait on me."

"Oh yes," she proclaimed. "You're a part of this family and we don't open presents until the whole family is here. So move your feet."

I laughed as she pushed me through the front door. Jackson picked me up and spun me around before both feet had even made it inside.

"I've missed you." He kissed my cheek.

"You just saw me last night." I replied, and kissed him lightly on the lips.

I suddenly realized that they were acting kind of weird. I felt like Jackson and Kennedy had some big secret that they were keeping from me, and that they were making hand signals or something behind my back.

It was weird. There was definitely something off.

Jackson tugged me along to the living room, where the rest of the family was sitting with big cheesy grins on their faces.

Yep, something was up.

I searched the room for some kind of a clue as to what was going on, but found nothing.

Except…

Under the tree were no presents. Kennedy had said just moments ago that there were tons of presents under the tree.

I squinted my eyes in her direction. "You little liar. What's going on?"

She just smiled but didn't say a word. Tucker walked into the room and swooped me up for a giant bear hug.

"They have a big surprise for you, but I'm not supposed to tell you." Tucker whispered in my ear. He really was a little rebel, but I loved that about him.

"Merry Christmas Tucker." I whispered back.

"Merry Christmas Gracie." He said loudly.

"I can't wait any longer." Nick jumped up from his lazy chair. He handed me a manila folder, kissed my cheek, and said, "Merry Christmas Gracie. We love you."

Just melt my heart like butter why don't ya?

"Open it," Kennedy bounced in excitement.

I sat down on the couch and slowly opened the envelope. There was a sheet of paper and a key inside.

I read the paper to myself not once, but twice. It couldn't be real. How was this possible? My eyes were wide as I scanned the room. Tears welled up in my eyes as I thought about what they had just done for me. I was speechless.

"Read it out loud Grace." Kennedy said to me.

"Miss Grace Dearman," I sniffled. "We have reviewed your application, and are pleased to announce your acceptance to Aurora Lane University for the 2016 spring semester. How did you guys know I applied? And how did you make it happen?" I cried.

"Don't you worry your pretty little head? It's done and you've got a bright future ahead of you. The year of two thousand sixteen, seventeen, eighteen, and nineteen will be paid in full."

"Four years." I jumped off the couch and nearly tackled Nick off his chair. "Thank you so much." I cried into his shoulder.

"You're welcome."

I hugged Claire too, and told her how wonderful she was. Their generous gift was beyond words.

"We gotta go shopping now, roomie." Kennedy pulled me to her side.

"Roomie?" I looked at her confused.

"The key silly. We have our own place. You and me are going to be partying it up." She knocked my hip against hers.

"No parties for me, but YAY to being roomies." I clapped.

"And this is why we love her." Claire said to Nick. They were talking about me. They thought I was a good influence for Kennedy, but truthfully she was a good girl all on her own.

"Come on, college student. I have a present for you." Jackson took my hand and led me out of the room. Tucker whistled at us as we left making me blush.

"Can you believe it Jackson? I'm going to school." An enormous smile was plastered on my face.

"Yes I can, and you're gonna do great." He said sweetly. "Merry Christmas."

He handed me small red box.

"We weren't supposed to buy gifts. I told you that."

"This is a different kind of gift, and I didn't buy it." He brushed a lock of hair from my face. "Open it."

I lifted the top off the beautiful red velvet box. "It's beautiful."

There was a small silver ring covered in a vine design.

"It was my Grandmother's ring. It's simple and beautiful, just like you." He took the ring out of the box. "I was hoping that you would wear it as a promise ring."

"A promise ring?" I asked.

"It will always remind you of my promises to you. My promise to always protect you, my promise to be your friend when you need one, and my promise to love you forever."

"I'm a lucky girl." I wrapped my arms around his neck and kissed his lips.

"Yes you are." He kissed me back. "I love you so much."

"I love you too."

Freedom is an amazing feeling, but freedom and love is above and beyond.

Acknowledgements

Can you believe it? This book is finally finished, and I feel like it has taken me forever. I've never more prouder of myself, because of the struggles with this book. This is the third time that I have come back to this story, and now it's finally finished. I can't believe. I guess 3rd time really is the charm. I hope you all loved it as much as me. Grace is pretty spectacular and I have wanted to tell her story for so long now.

There are tons of people to thank as always. I'm starting with my readers today. I have the greatest readers ever, and I have you to thank for each and every book that I write. I love you guys like crazy. Without you, this wouldn't be possible.

My supportive family at home who've been my rock, I love you guys. You are my life, and I am grateful to have you all. My husband and kids always support me one hundred percent, and that makes me a very lucky gal.

My Royals!!! Gosh, I love you girls. My royal street team is the best. They have supported me from day one, and they mean the world to me. Not only are they badass book pimps, but also they're also crown-wearing rock stars. Love you all.

Thank you Micalea Smeltzer. I know that I thank you in each and every book, and that you're probably sick of hearing it, but I truly don't know what I'd do without you. It's because of your support and your mad sprinting skills that this book was even finished. I owe you. You'll always be my most favorite partner in crime, and we'd look damn good in capes. Love you forever.

Beta Readers!!!! You know who you are. You've been by my side from the beginning and I can't thank you enough. All your hard work and time never go unnoticed. You're the best of the best. Thank you.

Last but not least, I have to thank my niece Kelsey Hellard. I dedicated this book to her, because she's so special to me. She was my very first niece. I still remember the day she was born. I was only ten years old. I've watched you grow up, and you've taught me so much. Probably more then I've taught you. The way you view life is a truly amazing gift, and I hope that more people will do the same. You see beauty in everything, and you have a kind heart, much like Grace. I love you Kels, and I thank you for being not just my family, but my friend.

About the Author

Regina is a contemporary romance writer from Kentucky. She lives there with her husband, dog, and cat. You can find her behind her computer, a good book, or watching sports. She loves to hear from her readers. Find out what's coming next by following her Facebook page at https://www.facebook.com/AuthReginaBartley?ref=hl !

More books by Regina Bartley

Continue reading for an excerpt of

The Road That Leads To Us

by Micalea Smeltzer

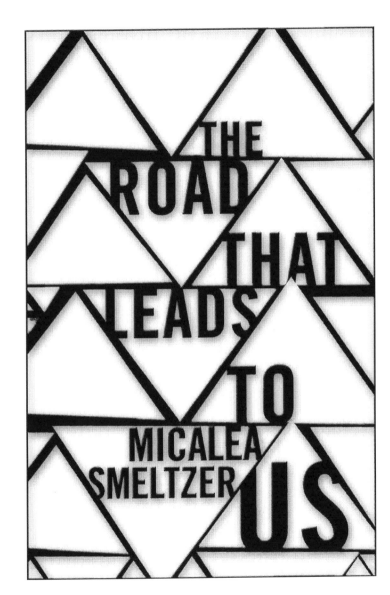

THE
ROAD
THAT
LEADS
TO
MICALEA
SMELTZER
US

Things are about to get rocky for Dean Wentworth and Willow Wade.

Willow Wade is used to living in the spotlight, with her father a famous drummer in the band Willow Creek—her namesake—it's been a lot to live up to and oftentimes she doesn't feel she's enough. But there has always been one person she could turn to.

Dean Wentworth knows a thing or two about how crippling a name can be. His family is worth billions after all. But Dean's always been content to do his own thing. Play his guitar. Work on cars. And geek out to his various "nerdoms".

But when Willow turns up unexpectedly, he realizes maybe there is more in life he wants.

Her.

One trip will change their lives forever.

ONE

Willow

Those bitches were gonna die.

That was a horrible thing to say about my so-called 'friends'—and I used the word friends loosely, because true friends wouldn't ditch you the day of your scheduled road trip because they'd rather be sunbathing in the Hamptons.

The fucking Hamptons.

Ew.

I mean, how clichéd could you get?

This was why I hated rich people.

It also sucked that I was one of those rich people.

Well, I wasn't, but my dad was.

So by extension so was I.

When you grew up with a rock star for a dad, cameras and eyes followed you everywhere. It was exhausting.

I couldn't just be Willow.

I was Willow Wade.

The daughter of the famous drummer Maddox Wade.

People expected greatness from me.

I just wanted to graduate college without slitting my wrists.

I fiddled with the radio, changing it to a country station—my dad would most definitely not approve—and let my blonde hair whip around my shoulders courtesy of the open windows.

The drive from NYU to my childhood home in Virginia was only about five hours, but it felt ten times longer thanks to the crazy traffic trying to get out of the city.

I might've yelled at a lot of people.

And waved my middle finger out the window.

My parents would be so proud.

Not.

My failed road trip might've been the reason I was headed home and not out west, but I was excited to be back where I grew up.

My freshman year of college had been trying, to say the least.

For most people college was their chance to spread their wings.

Me?

I found it oppressive.

That was probably due to the fact that I had no idea what I wanted to do with my life.

Did I want to act? Sing? Dance? Join a traveling circus?

I thought by going to NYU it would force me to finally decide what I wanted to do for the rest of my life.

If anything it only made me question everything that much more.

When the sprawling Victorian home came into view I couldn't stop the smile that split my face if I wanted to.

For the first time since I left last August, I could finally breathe.

I was home.

I parked my car in the driveway and hopped out—pulling in a healthy lungful of clean mountain air.

So much better than the exhaust fume-filled air that littered New York City.

I grabbed my patchwork backpack from the passenger seat and slung it over my shoulder.

Slipping my sunglasses off my face and into my hair I headed for the front door.

I pulled the key from my pocket, rubbing my thumb against the worn hedgehog key cap.

I entered the home and nearly cried at the rush of familiarity.

I was still majorly bummed that my plans for a road trip hadn't worked out, and I'd probably mope about it for a week in a bout of teenage angst, but being home wasn't all that bad.

I'd missed my house.

My parents.

My siblings.

And even the hedgehogs.

My dad had a thing for hedgehogs, so by extension I guess I did too. They were pretty cute.

The house was eerily quiet as I stepped inside and I looked around for my brother Mascen and my sister Lylah.

Neither was anywhere to be seen.

I moved further into the house, skimming my fingers over the familiar pale yellow walls on my way to the kitchen.

No one appeared to be home and I needed food.

Humming softly under my breath I rounded the corner into the spacious kitchen and immediately regretted my destination.

"MY EYES!" I screamed, slapping a hand over my eyes. "My poor innocent eyes!" I gagged for added effect.

Catching my mom and dad making out in the kitchen like a couple of teenagers had not been on my to-do list for the day.

Neither had seeing my mom's bra or my dad's hand skimming up her skirt.

I turned around, walking away as fast as my feet would carry me. "I'm going to go throw up now!"

I heard them shuffling in the kitchen, no doubt righting their clothes.

Thank God there had been no exposed body parts.

I might've been traumatized for life.

"Willow!" I heard my mom call my name, but I was already headed for the stairs. "We didn't know you were coming home."

"Yeah, I kinda sorta forgot to call on my way out of hell," I muttered under my breath, hurrying up the steps.

"Willow." She called again and this time her voice was close.

I paused on the stairs and turned to find her standing at the bottom of the staircase with her hands on her hips.

"Are you okay, honey?" A wrinkle marred her brow.

With her wild and untamable blonde hair, kind blue eyes, and boho chic style, my mom was still a knockout at forty-one years old.

"Just dandy."

She narrowed her eyes on me. "Spill it, I know you're lying."

Groaning, I stomped up the rest of the stairs. "I don't want to talk about it."

I headed down the hall and up the attic stairs to my bedroom.

I knew my mom was following, but I acted like I didn't notice.

Kicking off my black and white Chucks I belly flopped onto my gray and yellow paisley bedspread. Wrapping my arms around the pillow I inhaled the familiar scent of the lavender fabric softener my mom always used.

The bed dipped near my feet.

"What happened, sweetie?" She asked.

I rolled over onto my back and frowned. "Everything."

"Talking about it will probably make you feel better."

"And so will this tea."

I smiled at the sound of my dad's voice as he appeared in the doorway of my room.

"Hi, dad."

"Hey, princess."

I might've been nineteen years old now, but I would always be my daddy's princess.

He handed me one of the cups of tea and gave the other to my mom.

Pulling out the fluffy white swivel desk chair he took a seat and clasped his hands together.

"We weren't expecting you home."

I snorted. "I kinda figured that out. I'm sorry. I should've called. Where are Mascen and Lylah?" I looked around like they might suddenly jump out from behind my bed.

He chuckled. "They're still in school. The high school hasn't let out for the summer yet."

"Oh, right," I mumbled, having forgotten that my college courses ended before their schedule did.

"What happened with your road trip?" My mom asked.

"My friends are a bunch of cunt waffles."

"Willow!" She admonished. "That's not nice."

"They're not nice," I reasoned. Waving my arms dramatically, I began to explain my tragic tale. "I showed up at Lauren's apartment, where I was supposed to pick her and Greta up—and someone please explain to me who the hell would name their child Greta. I mean, honestly."

"Willow," my mom warned.

She said my name a lot.

She even had different ways of saying it.

So I'd know when I was in trouble, or she was irritated.

She was definitely irritated at the moment.

Me interrupting her and my dad about to go at it like a couple of rabbits probably added to that—not just my tendency to ramble endlessly.

"Sorry," I said, even though I wasn't really sorry. "Anyway, I get there, and I'm knocking on the door, and I'm all like, 'Let's gooooo my kemo-sabes!' and then Lauren opens the door dressed in a robe. A robe. And informs me that they've changed their minds and roughing it isn't appealing. Instead, they're going to the Hamptons because Greta's parents have a place there beside Ryan Goosling or whatever his name is." I paused, pulling in a lungful of air. "I just don't understand who in their right mind would pass up a road trip in order to sunbathe and spy on a guy with a name that sounds like goose."

My parents stared at me and then their eyes slid to each other.

They both looked like they were fighting laughter at my pain.

Jerks.

I lifted the cup of tea to my lips and winced at the taste before setting the mug on the bedside table.

My dad, he tried, but he could not make tea to save himself.

"Princess, not everyone's like you."

"What's that supposed to mean?" I bristled.

He chuckled. "Simmer down, Tiger. All I'm saying is, you're adventurous. A sedentary life isn't for you. Most people aren't like that. They're afraid to put themselves out there into the unknown, but you're not."

"Are you saying I should join the traveling circus? Because that idea is looking more appealing every day."

"Nah," he laughed and leaned forward to tap his finger against my toe, "I'd miss you too much. Sending you off to college was bad enough."

I frowned at the mention of college.

"What is it?" My mom asked softly, picking up on the sudden shift in me. She was perceptive like that.

I shrugged, picking up one of the many throw pillows on my bed and hugged it to my chest.

"Nothing," I lied. "I'm just tired and cranky."

She looked at me doubtfully. "Are you sure that's it?"

I nodded.

I knew my mom and dad wouldn't care if I threw my hands up and said college wasn't for me. But that was the thing. I didn't know that. I was completely and utterly clueless. Maybe college was for me and I was just at the wrong one.

Or maybe it wasn't.

I didn't know.

And I was afraid I never would.

I was terrified of graduating from college with a degree in something I didn't even like and being stuck.

Stuck and Willow Wade did not go well together.

But it was hard to explain to anyone, especially my parents, what I wanted when I didn't even know.

Maybe, this summer, I'd get my shit together and figure my life out.

Not likely, but one could hope.

My parents looked at me with pity in their eyes.

They knew I was full of shit but they were too nice to call me on it—for now at least.

Jumping up from my bed I slipped my feet back into my shoes.

"I'm going to head out for a while. I'll be back for dinner."

"Don't you want to finish your tea?" My dad asked.

I tried not to gag. "Nope, I'm good. Y'all just...uh...get back to whatever it was you were about to do before I got here."

I only made it to the door before I stopped, horrified. Swiftly turning around, I pointed a finger at them. "But don't do that on my bed, because that's just gross and weird on so many levels. Go to your own room."

My dad bellowed out a laugh but quickly sobered. "You don't need to leave because of us."

"I know," I replied, "I just need to get out."

Before either of them could stop me I bound down the stairs and out the door.

I was slightly out of breath by the time I reached my car.

I should probably work out more.

Nah, who was I kidding? That was never going to happen...unless balancing a Cheeto on the top of your lip counted as exercise because then I was totally ahead of the game.

I slid back into the car, my sore bum protesting at this fact, and headed into town.

I wasn't sure where I was going, and I ended up stopping at the local coffee shop/restaurant, Griffin's, for some food.

Armed with a coffee and muffin, I suddenly knew where I needed to go.

Well, more like who I needed to see.

Cramming half the muffin in my mouth and getting crumbs all over myself—so ladylike, I know—I hurried from Griffin's out into the warm sunshine.

Behind the wheel of my car once more I headed to my new destination.

When the building came into sight my lips lifted into one of the biggest grins I'd worn in a long time and I hadn't even seen him yet.

I parked my car at the side of the building and walked around to the open garage door.

Wentworth Wheels was emblazoned on the front of the building and inside several mechanics bustled around. They laughed and chatted loudly as they worked—trying to be heard above the sounds of their tools.

I stepped inside, inhaling the familiar scent of oil and rubber. Most people hated that smell, but I loved it. It brought back so many memories.

I craned my neck around, looking for familiar floppy brown hair, but he wasn't to be seen.

And then, there he was.

He came out from the back office, wiping down a piece of metal with a red rag.

When he looked up he saw me and a grin that matched my own lit his face.

Barreling forward I ran into his arms.

He caught me immediately and spun me around.

"Dean," I breathed against his neck, hugging him tight.

I'd missed him so much.

Dean Wentworth was my best friend.

We'd grown up together—his dad was the cousin of the guitar player in my dad's band—and he was one of the few people I could turn to with anything. His parents might not have been famous, but they had a lot of money, so he could relate to many of the same things I went through. I was also close with his younger sister, Grace, but my connection to Dean was stronger.

Sometimes there were people that just got each other, and that's how it was with us.

Setting me down he placed the piece of metal on a nearby worktable and tucked the rag in the back pocket of his jeans before crossing his arms over his chest.

"Willow Wade in the flesh." He looked me up and down. "I feel like I haven't seen you in forever."

"It's been a while," I conceded.

I hadn't seen Dean since New Year's when I'd attended his family's annual party. It was kind of a big deal and not to be missed.

I hadn't talked to him much there because his girlfriend had been with him.

She was an insufferable bitch that I wanted to gag and toss over a bridge into a lake.

He could do so much better.

"How's Brooklyn?" I sneered her name.

I'd tried to be nice to her when they first started dating last summer, but she made her distaste of me obvious—I was too loud, too crazy, and far too opinionated for her.

"Wouldn't know. We broke up in February."

I clucked my tongue. "You got her the wrong chocolate for Valentine's day, didn't you?"

He laughed fully at that. "Probably. We just weren't a good match. She kept trying to hide my Pokémon cards and that wasn't cool."

By now the other mechanics were staring at us with interest. I recognized a few of them and waved.

"Come on," Dean nodded towards the open garage door, "let's head up to the apartment to talk."

"You're not going to get in trouble are you?"

"I know the owner." He winked, referring to his dad.

My Chucks squeaked against the concrete floor as I followed Dean through the garage, outside, and around the side of the building to the set of stairs that led to the apartment above the shop. Dean was nearly two years older than me, and as soon as he graduated high school he'd moved in here and gotten his certificate to be a mechanic. He'd known from the time he was three and could hold a wrench that he wanted to be a mechanic like his dad. If only I was that lucky.

Dean swung the door open and waved me inside.

It looked much the way I remembered—muted gray walls, black leather furniture, and old-timey western and sci-fi movie posters on the wall.

"Thirsty?" Dean asked, already moving into the small kitchen.

I slid onto one of the red leather barstools and nodded.

He opened the fridge and seemed to be searching for something. Finally, he pulled out a glass bottle of Orange Crush soda.

"Ah!" I squealed, reaching out with grabby hands. "I can't believe you still get these!"

"'Course," he shrugged, unscrewing the cap on another and leaning across the counter towards me, "they're your favorite."

"I haven't had one of these in forever." I gulped greedily at it.

"They don't have Orange Crush soda in New York City?" He questioned with a raised brow.

"I'm sure they do," I relented, rubbing the condensation off the glass with my thumb, "but not in a glass bottle. Plus, I wouldn't be able to have it with you. This is our thing."

He grinned at that. "I've missed you, Will."

"Bleh," I gagged, "I wish that nickname would die already. I have a vagina, therefore I'm not a Will."

He chuckled and leaned his head back, swallowing a large gulp of the soda. "I've missed you, Willow," he amended.

"Much better."

"I've got somethin' else for you." He began shuffling through a kitchen drawer. When he found whatever it was he was looking for he exclaimed, "Aha!"

He held the blue raspberry lollipop out for me with a crooked smile. "Been saving all of these for you."

"My momma always told me not to take candy from a stranger," I quipped, taking the lollipop anyway—there was no way I was passing up blue raspberry. It was my favorite.

"Guess it's a good thing I'm not a stranger." He winked.

I unwrapped the lollipop and stuck it in my mouth. "Mmm," I hummed, "that's good."

He laughed and grabbed one for himself. Sour apple.

We grew quiet for a moment, and then he broke the silence. "This feels good. It feels like you never left."

I sighed, looking down at the worn ends of my shoes. "I wish I'd never left," I muttered.

"Is it really that bad?" He asked. "College, I mean."

I pulled the lollipop from my mouth. "I don't know whether it's college or me."

"Ah, I see." He nodded.

"You know me," I continued, "I hate being confined. I thought once I graduated high school I'd be free to wander the world and do what I wanted, but then I felt like I needed to go to school, and maybe it is what I need but it's not what I want."

"So...maybe you take next year off," he suggested.

"But I don't know if that's what I want. That's the problem. I'm so confused."

"What's something you do want?" The white end of the lollipop stuck out between his lips.

"Well," I slid the barstool back and kicked my feet up on the counter, "I wanted to go on a road trip and my so-called friends bailed. Assholes." I muttered the last part under my breath.

He chuckled, crossing his arms over his chest. "Because you're such a delight to hang out with twenty-four-seven."

I stuck my now blue tongue out at him.

Sobering, he walked around and sat on the empty barstool beside me. "Why don't we go on a road trip?"

My eyes widened in surprise. "Me and you?"

"Sure, why not?" He shrugged, crunching down on his lollipop and chewing the candy. "I mean, we're friends, I just finished restoring my Mustang, and getting out of here for a little while wouldn't be the worst thing ever."

"Would your dad let you take off work for that long? My plan was to head south and then west all the way to California to visit Liam," I said, referring to my cousin who was only a few months older than me and like a brother, "and then come back up the northern route."

"My dad won't care." Dean shrugged, tossing the lollipop stick in the direction of the trashcan. It hit the edge and bounced off. Dean never had much aim. It was a good thing he stuck to fixing cars and playing music. I didn't think he went anywhere without his guitar.

Excitement flooded my body, nearly bubbling over.

"Are you sure?" I asked him one last time.

"Positive."

"We're really going to do this?"

He nodded.

"Thank you!" I squealed, nearly falling to the floor in my haste to hug him.

"Whoa," he grunted in surprise when my body collided into his. He wrapped his arms around me, hugging me back.

"Thank you, thank you, thank you!" I said a thousand more times before smacking a kiss against his stubbled cheek. "This is going to be epic."

Before he could respond, I was out the door and down the steps.

I had a road trip to pack for.

49201465R00176

Made in the USA
Charleston, SC
20 November 2015